Mischief in Moonstone Series, Novella 4:
When the Dead People Brought a Dish-to-Pass

By Christine DeSmet

Writers Exchange E-Publishing
http://www.writers-exchange.com

Mischief in Moonstone Series, Novella 4: When the Dead People Brought a Dish-to-Pass

Copyright 2018, 2023, 2025 Christine DeSmet

Writers Exchange E-Publishing

PO Box 372

ATHERTON QLD 4883

Cover Art by: Jatin and Sandy Cummins

Published by Writers Exchange E-Publishing

http://www.writers-exchange.com

Chapter 1

The car crash echoed all the way up Porcupine Hill. Its bone-crunching wallop rattled the kitchen windows, uprooting Alyssa Swain from gluing down new floor tiles.

She held her breath, listening, paying respects. She knew. Ever since moving into the farmhouse atop the hill a few miles south of Moonstone, Wisconsin two months ago, she'd endured screaming car brakes as drivers descended the fifty-yard drop into the hairpin turn. She knew somebody had finally died.

With hands shaking and heart pumping, Alyssa pulled a stocking cap over her short-cropped, brown hair. She grabbed the yellow barn coat and leather gloves from a wood peg by the kitchen door. After reaching for the doorknob, she hesitated. Blood bathed her memory. There would be too much blood this time, too. She knew.

When a feathery whip hit her legs her breath caught again. For a moment she thought it some ethereal force telling her to stop her heinous nightmare visits to the past.

Alyssa looked down. Her lungs whooshed out pent-up air. "Millicent, please, I'm in a hurry."

The white Angora cat blinked up with one gold eye and one blue before untangling herself from Alyssa's legs.

After calling 911, Alyssa flung herself into whirlwinds of brown, red, and gold leaves on the crisp October Thursday. She raced down the short gravel driveway then onto the black-topped county road, following it the few yards to the crest of the hill. Far below, fingers of fog reached out of Red Rock Creek, wending through the woodland to huff hoary mist at an upside down, midnight blue car. The car had smashed head-on into a birch tree, its triad of white trunks bent over the car like a mother flailing arms over a dead baby.

Alyssa's mind spun. If only she had slowed down that day...

If only. That's our punishment after such things happen. We live our lives in "if only" limbo. Even after four years.

She ran hells bells down the blacktop grade. Tears flowed, wicked away by air that spiked colder as she descended into the lowland.

If I can get there faster this time maybe I can save--

Red rivulets drizzled down the upside down window frame then onto an aqua explosion of glass pebbles decorating damp, gold leaves. Alyssa fought the urge to retch. She crouched within arm's length of a man hanging upside down in his seat belt.

"Hello?" The simple question was all she could muster while holding onto her stomach.

Blood oozed off strands of his black hair and chin. A massive shoulder encased in a camouflage jacket was wedged against the door frame. He lay twisted with his face toward her. The deflating air bag cradled a cheek. Dark eyes were open but still as a brackish marsh pool, unnerving her. "Are you all right, sir?"

Nothing.

Alyssa shot up. She listened for the EMTs. No sirens yet. Nothing.

She threw herself at the steep hill, angry for impulsively running down the hill instead of driving her truck with its first aid kit and blanket. She stopped twice because her lungs seized.

Finally she leaped into her Jeep Cherokee, chiding herself again. Last time she'd left the rescue to the EMTs. She couldn't do that again. *"Mrs. Swain, the EMTs did the best they could but I'm sorry to have to tell you..."*

Alyssa had barely turned around in her driveway when a shiny, new squad car pulled alongside her. A woman in a brown uniform and jacket, with a blonde ponytail pulled through a baseball-style regulation cap, got out.

Alyssa rolled down her window. "He's all right? The ambulance came already?"

"Did you hear anything odd?"

Why weren't they racing to help the man? "A crash."

"But no brakes, right?"

She hadn't heard the usual squeal of brakes on the hill. She swallowed. Had the man meant to run into the trees to commit suicide? "No, Officer, I didn't hear brakes."

"Please call me Lily."

Alyssa wanted to scream. *Why are we wasting time?* Her hands trembled on the wheel. "Lily, is he--?"

"I'm afraid..."

"They tried their best, Mrs. Swain." Alyssa choked. She hadn't been able to save the man in the car either. She turned off the truck engine.

"Ma'am?" Officer Lily tapped her arm. "Ma'am?"

"I'm sorry. I knew he died. I knew. I saw it in his eyes, but I was hoping--"

"There is no dead man."

"He's alive?"

"We didn't find anybody."

"But you found the car? It was smashed. He'd rolled it."

"Maybe he was smashed and walked away to avoid a ticket. There's nobody at the bottom of the hill. I'll have the car towed into town. It's a BMW. Not from around here."

Alyssa got out of the truck to run to her barbed wire fence. She followed it until the crest of the hill. The car was still held in the arms of the birch tree. She called back to the officer, "He was there, unconscious, bloody. He couldn't've walked away."

"Maybe he wore a red scarf and you just thought you saw blood."

Alyssa raced back to the officer. "No, he was wearing camouflage, nothing red. He was bleeding. It covered his face and was all over the broken window glass. Did you look in the creek? Maybe he crawled out and fell into the water."

Officer Lily placed a reassuring hand on Alyssa's arm. "It's Halloween week. It was a joke by high school kids playing hooky. I'm the new deputy here so I've been expecting something like this. They probably stole the wreck from a junkyard, stuffed a dummy in it with fake blood, and now they'll be watching the papers for news of the wreck. That is, if I put this silliness into a report." Lily giggled. "Not!"

Unease wouldn't loosen its strangle-hold on Alyssa's sixth sense. The man had been real. She was sure of it. But the pony-tailed deputy shrugged at her.

Alyssa managed a smile. "Yeah, it was probably a trick." She hated Halloween. The horrible accident she'd lived through four years before had happened on the holiday that celebrated dead souls.

"I'm Alyssa Swain. I'm a new dealer at the Port Cliff casino."

Lily shook her hand. "You must work with a friend of mine, Claire Lone Eagle. Her husband's building a gazebo behind the North Pole."

"North Pole?"

Lily laughed, an unexpected sound that relaxed Alyssa despite herself. "That's what they call the Victorian mansion in Moonstone that overlooks

Lake Superior. It has a restaurant called The Jingle Bell Inn run by another friend of mine, Kirsten. She's expanding it with an enclosed aviary, an outdoor deck, fire pit and heated gazebo. She wants it all done before the wedding."

"Sounds like a big shindig."

"A Christmas wedding for Peter LeBarron. His father, Henri, owns the mansion. Peter's marrying Crystal Hagan, known for her pet reindeer, alpaca, and goats. She teaches first grade."

First grade. Alyssa shivered again so violently that she had to excuse herself to throw up.

After assuring the deputy she'd be fine, she went to the house and crawled into bed.

A menacing rapping downstairs made her sit up with her heartbeat skittering like fall leaves. But she had to have dreamed the knocking. Millicent slept curled in a white ball next to her. The white cat always leapt down to hide under the bed when anybody came to the door.

The knocks came harder. Banging. Urgent.

"Damn kids." Alyssa suspected she'd get down to the door to find nothing. But why wasn't Millicent awakened by the noise? Alyssa scrutinized her watch-cat. Her fur moved; she was breathing.

Alyssa slipped into her shearling-lined moccasins and fuzzy lavender robe, cinching it tight. She grabbed her cell phone...her thumb ready for the 911 speed button.

Downstairs she found nothing at the living room's front door but cold air nipping at her bare ankles. She sighed, certain now that it was a trick. Sure enough, sharp raps came next from the kitchen.

She rushed through the hall, minced carefully around the tiles and tools on the kitchen floor, then opened the door. "Yeah, yeah, trick or treat--"

It was him. The dead man.

Alyssa went light-headed at the sight of the tall, black-haired man filling her doorway, giving her a lopsided grin. His eyes were the rich brown color called burnt sienna, part of the palette of stains she was using to refurbish the woodwork. He wore the camouflage jacket but it sported no blood. His hair was combed in neat waves from a side part.

"Can I help you?" she asked. How had he cleaned up so fast? Maybe her cat hadn't moved because this was a dream. The man wore spotless, indigo blue denims and high leather boots with leather laces. He carried an overloaded toolbox.

"Where do you want me to start?"

She clutched the bathrobe together at her neck. "Pardon me?"

"We've got a lot to do before Sunday."

"What's Sunday? Who are you?" Had she forgotten about hiring a carpenter? Certainly thirty-five was too young to be that forgetful.

"Your Halloween party for all your dead relatives."

She wasted no time in slamming the door on the lunatic's face.

She locked the door. If the man knocked, she would punch 911.

Millicent padded into the kitchen as if nobody had been at the door. She didn't sniff the air as she usually did with disturbances. Instead, she picked her way to her glass bowl of kibble near the refrigerator.

Alyssa tiptoed to the window next to the door. She peeked around the green-and-white striped cotton curtains she'd hung only yesterday. She saw nobody in the driveway or near the barn northwest of the house. The barn was locked, so she felt safe that he wasn't hiding there.

Alyssa shook her head, smiling. She was groggy, overly-tired from trying to refurbish a house over a hundred years old. She'd dreamed everything.

She had barely turned from the window when the tall man walked through the door.

As in, he walked through the closed...locked...solid walnut door.

Alyssa stumbled backward.

"How did you do that?" She slapped her face to wake up. "I get it. A Halloween trick. You're a hologram?" She looked around him expecting to see somebody projecting a light through the window over the sink. But she didn't see anybody.

The tall man with broad shoulders stood in the middle of her kitchen, toolbox in hand, shaking his head, nonplussed at the room. "Don't tell me you were thinking you could strip that wallpaper, refinish that tin ceiling and these floors by Sunday? Are the other rooms as bad?"

Alyssa lunged the two long steps to the kitchen table to snatch a chair to use as a weapon. "How did you get in here?"

He shrugged. "I walked through the door. Isn't that how most people do it?"

"But, but--" She shook the chair at him as she scuttled to the door. She put the chair down to feel the door. "This door is locked. You have a key?"

He put the toolbox on the counter, giving her an eyeful of a denim-clad backside. He wore a hammer to the side like suggestive jewelry. She blinked in confusion while he brushed the countertop with a broad hand. "Cheap gray linoleum replete with cigarette burns. You smoke?"

She grabbed for the chair again. "Of course not. And do I look like the kind who'd set her cigarette directly on the countertop?"

His dark gaze flicked up and down her. "No. You look a little uptight actually. Either that or you're a lion tamer. Damn sexy one, I might add."

Her insides fluttered, first in embarrassment, then in frustration. She must have hired him, yet she had no recollection of it. To her dismay, he stood between her and the cell phone she'd left on the counter. She excused herself to go upstairs to toss on armor: a grubby, gray fleece sweatshirt and pants covered with tiling cement, wood stain, and white ceiling paint. She took a fortifying breath before trotting back down to the kitchen.

He'd hung his jacket over a chair back and was rolling up the sleeves of a blue work shirt to reveal tanned arms with sprinkles of dark hair. She hadn't noticed how tan he was earlier at the accident scene. If this were even the same man. The tawny color softened the weathered face but made the glint in his dark eyes all the brighter by contrast.

Alyssa's belly did a flip-flop. The light in his eyes reminded her of a tunnel connecting two worlds. She wanted to climb in and see where the tunnel would take her.

He said, "Where should we start? Here or upstairs in the bedroom?"

She picked up a chair again.

With a weary sigh, he snatched it and set it aside. "Could you move over that way a little?" He pointed toward the striped curtains.

"Why?"

"You're blocking the door and my cat, Dillinger, wants to come in."

For some odd reason she obeyed. A huge, shaggy, matted, brown-and-copper ring-tailed cat with one milky, blind eye materialized through the walnut door. It paused, hissed like a panther, then pawed at a cocklebur stuck to one ear.

"Get that fleabag out of here!" Alyssa leaped between the scruffy cat and her white Angora still eating next to the refrigerator.

"They'll be fine," the man said, leaning near Alyssa to retrieve for his toolbox.

He smelled pleasant, like the fog before it evaporated in the late morning sun. Alyssa's mouth went dry. She backed up against the vibrating refrigerator. She was ready to scoop up Millicent, but the man was right about the cats. Millicent crunched away on kibble, oblivious to the rogue cat. *Millicent, run! Hide as usual! That's a vicious wild cat!*

The man shook her hand, shaking Alyssa out of her reverie. His touch was like nothing she'd ever experienced. It made her body melt like chocolate left on a steam radiator. She seemed to merge with him, settling into a soft pool of comfort. Somehow she heard him saying, "Name's John Christopherson. Nice to meet you, Alyssa Swain."

How did he know her name? She couldn't blame this memory loss on a night of drinking. She didn't drink alcohol. She was about to start though.

"When did I hire you?"

He walked through the plaster wall between the kitchen and hallway, then came back to stand in the real doorway. Alyssa winced. "How did you do that? And how do you know who I am?"

His face darkened. "Let's just say that I was commissioned to come here."

"What does that mean?" His cat hissed, baring fangs at Alyssa. "Put that wild thing outside."

"He's had a bad night. We both have. We'll work it off."

"No, you won't." Her boldness made her heartbeat quicken. "I don't care who commissioned you. Oh crap, my ex-husband didn't hire you, did he? Get out."

His cat snarled, pawing at the air with threatening talons.

Alyssa shivered. "What is wrong with that mangy thing?"

John brightened, as if glad for the change in subject. "Can't you hear it?"

"Hear what?"

"Your toilet's running. Dillinger picks up on irritating sounds. I'll have it fixed in a jiffy for you. The ball cock is probably corroded. Nothing worse than a rusty cock."

She was sure she'd turned flame red. John winked before clomping down the hallway. He and his cat took the staircase two steps at a time.

She rushed to the bottom of the stairs, waiting like a ninny. The toilet tank lid clanked. Everything sounded real up there. The man was humming a song that was vaguely familiar. *"Moon River, wider than a mile..."*

Alyssa hurried to the kitchen to use the cell phone. She whispered, "Deputy Lily? It's Alyssa Swain. Hurry. I have an intruder."

"Where is he now?"

"Fixing my toilet."

Silence. Then a giggle. "I'm betting this is all Tootsie's doings. Her 'Welcome Wagon' approach. We have a crazy woman called Tootsie Winters who loves to stick her nose in other people's business. She raises silkie chickens. Were there any lavender chickens running around with the man? She's trying to unload new chicks hatched in September."

"No. Just a really bad-looking cat with one eye and lots of attitude."

"A man who likes cats can't be dangerous. But I'll come check him out."

About a half hour later, Alyssa was pacing in her kitchen listening to John using an electric sander on the wood floor in the living room. When Deputy Lily arrived, she dashed past John to open the front door.

A blast of wind howled, whipping brown oak leaves in with the officer.

John kept on working on the floors, paying them no attention.

Lily took off her cap. She re-did her ponytail. "That's some wind. We're going to get snow for Halloween, I hear."

By the way Lily smiled at Alyssa expectantly, Alyssa knew the deputy couldn't see John or hear the sander's whining. But Alyssa had to try. "You don't hear anything?"

"Who can hear anything over that howl outside?"

"You don't see anything?"

Lily peered at the smooth, maple wood floor. "You've been busy. That floor is gorgeous. You sand it yourself?"

Alyssa sagged. "I guess I must've." Under John's firm fists the sander whirred in a corner.

"Now where's this guy with the cat?"

She gave up. "He left. Sorry to bother you." Before Lily could leave, though, Alyssa grabbed the deputy's coat sleeve. It felt real.

Lily smiled. "Something else?"

"You're sure you don't see anything? A man with broad shoulders? Wavy head of black hair? Denims that fit, well, nice, with a hammer in a loop?"

"Tootsie Winters got to you, didn't she? This house isn't haunted, no matter what she says."

"Haunted?" Alyssa had her share of bad dreams. She didn't need to add to them.

"I guess she didn't tell you. Keep in mind Tootsie is the former mayor's wife, but she still thinks she's running the town. She tries to create lore to bring in the tourists. According to her, this house is an in-between house."

"What does that mean?"

"I don't know. I'm a facts person. Tootsie's the kind to read the Duluth-Superior obits then insist those ghosts pass through here for your great view of Lake Superior."

Alyssa paled. If the woman read obituaries for entertainment, did she know about Alyssa's little girl? Alyssa choked on anger. Had this Tootsie hired somebody to taunt her, to punish her for what had happened four years ago this weekend?

"I need to be alone. I'm not feeling well." Alyssa hoped Lily would forgive her for practically shoving her out the front door. This was twice she'd taken ill in the presence of the officer.

John stopped the sander. He flashed a smile. "So how's it look?"

Alyssa was so mad she could barely make her teeth unclench. "You're a cruel person. Who put you up to this sick joke?"

He came to her in swift strides, cupping her elbows in the palms of his broad hands. Heat rippled from him like a warm wave on a beach at sunset, lapping into her body, buoying her.

"It's not a joke." The tunnel of light widened, inviting her again. "I know about your daughter and how she died. That's why I'm here. The police report was wrong. You didn't mean to kill little Sadie Rose."

Chapter 2

Whether she was finally going mad from guilt, or this was some nightmare punishment for her hand in her daughter's death, Alyssa couldn't discern. Did it matter? Her daughter had died because of Alyssa.

She sank shivering into the living room couch. "So you're a detective? My ex's attorney? An insurance agent wanting your money back? Did you pay too much for my daughter?"

John sat beside her. "I'm really a carpenter. And I'm here to help you figure out the best way to memorialize Sadie Rose."

A hunger overwhelming her defied common sense. She wanted him to be real. When he entwined his fingers with hers, all she could feel was a cushion of heat and not the details of muscle, knuckles, and skin. "You know something about the accident that I don't?"

"I'm here because your daughter can't reach you."

The distrust in him returned. "Of course she can't. She's dead."

"But that's all she is. She's waiting for your help."

"What're you talking about?" He had to be an actor. This *was* a Halloween trick. Alyssa got up from the couch to eye him with suspicion.

John leaned forward, kneading his hands. "She can't move on to her proper place in the afterlife until you move on without her."

"I can't forget her. I'm her mother." Tears clouded her vision.

"You need to find a way to send her away. You're holding onto her so tightly that she can't even play along the river."

"What river?"

"The river she's waiting in line to cross."

She recalled the song he'd hummed earlier. "Oh puh-lease. Who hired you to put on this show?"

"Doesn't matter." Wrinkles settled in his rugged face again. "Perhaps I can get Sadie Rose to talk to you at the party about this issue."

"For the last time, there's no party. No dead people are coming to my house this Sunday."

"I'm afraid they are. I know for sure your great-great Grandmother Sadie is coming. She was hoping you'd make the pumpkin tarts you do so well."

Alyssa flinched. How did John Christopherson know about the pumpkin tarts? And her daughter's namesake?

"The tarts sound good," John said in a smooth tone.

"I haven't made them for four years." *Not since the accident. The accident happened because of my damn cooking!* Her hands grew clammy. John wouldn't understand. "I don't cook anymore. Please, we can't have a party."

"Ah, because you were a caterer. You're sick of cooking. I have the solution. We'll make it a dish-to-pass party. Everybody brings their specialty to share."

"How can dead people bring a dish-to-pass? They're dead."

John leaned back on the sofa, a smug smile spreading wide. "The in-between allows dead people to do whatever they did in the few days before their death. They just can't do anything new until they go on to the after-life."

Trying to process that, Alyssa sank onto one end of the couch again. "So you're saying my great-great grandmother is still cooking on her wood stove?"

"Yes. It's rather smoky in the in-between at times."

"And my great-great grandfather is still chopping wood in the timberlands and hauling it in for her, along with water from a well and a fresh kill for the meal?"

John winced. "I'm afraid not."

"That was supposed to be a joke." After he shrugged, she asked, "Well, where is he?"

"It seems he was having an affair--?"

"You can't possibly know that."

"Want to know how he died? He was apologizing to your great-great grandmother for the affair, and when they were having makeup sex he had his heart attack. The apology took their relationship back to its original form, which allowed him to pass directly to Heaven."

"Because he had an affair?" Alyssa rubbed her temples. This was a doozy of a dream. "So great sex gets you into Heaven?"

"No, he got there because he returned things to their original way. He apologized and your grandma forgave him. When we make things right again, that's when we truly hear the voices of our loved ones and can move forward and be happy."

"You're not going to make me relive my daughter's accident."

With a sick feeling climbing up her throat, Alyssa raced through the kitchen and out the door, stumbling to nowhere, hugging her sweatshirt against the bitter wind.

John's warm aura soon enveloped her as they stood looking at the strip of Lake Superior. "I'm here to help you get this old place returned to its original condition by Sunday. If you make things right in this house again, if you restore it to its original beauty, then you'll have a chance to hear your daughter's voice. This house is nothing less than the re-start of your life."

Alyssa could swear his heat was real. But dreams often felt real. "I'll get to talk with my daughter?"

"She needs to tell you the words you didn't hear after the accident happened and just before she died."

Her heart stopped. "She said something? In the ambulance?" *She needed me? And I wasn't there at the final moment?*

"That's what I've been told."

Feeling herself sinking into this game, she asked, "When I hear her, will she be two years old still? Or six?"

"She's two. She'll always be two while waiting to move on."

An ache scraped at Alyssa. She couldn't bear thinking about her daughter stuck in time. Could the party for the dead on Sunday really rectify this? Impossible. But what if it could? Would she have the strength to endure whatever this party brought? John promised she wouldn't have to relive the accident, but Alyssa saw disaster looming. Her guilt could grow even more powerful, pulling her toward an abyss.

She shivered. "Am I going to see my daughter in addition to hearing her?"

"I don't know. It's her choice."

"Is she angry with me?"

John's face clouded. "That's between you and her."

"You said she plays. Then she must be happy."

"She seems sad when she plays. She plays alone. That's what I've seen."

Alyssa's heartbeat banged in her ears as she looked up into his penetrating eyes. "You really came here to help me and my daughter. But I don't see how a tater-tot casserole will change everything."

"You will." He leaned down, his mouth pressing heat on her lips.

She reached up to touch his black, wavy hair, but her fingers collected only the breeze. She backed off. "Let's go inside. You must be cold without a coat."

He chuckled. "That's a good one."

After they went inside and she locked the kitchen door, the wind roared like a tornado, shaking the old house. Alyssa had to grab the counter. Plaster dust puffed off the walls. "What was that?"

"Your relatives. They're trying to get in."

"They walk through walls, too?"

He shrugged.

Ordinarily dreamland adventures evaporated during the day, but the promise of hearing her daughter's final words created a new urgency for Alyssa to believe in the power of dreams. She'd always used physical work to help her sleep well, to get past the nasty dreams, the ones with the neon headline: *Car rolls; child dies.* But now she found herself wanting to believe in John, in the dead relatives, the party, and above all the dream that might contain her daughter. Alyssa wanted to crawl back inside her dreams for the first time in four years. She wanted to crawl inside John's eyes. She wanted him to be real.

But John didn't know that Alyssa's biggest flaw was her headlong rush through life. She'd purchased this rundown house to rectify her big flaw-- impulsiveness. She wanted to force herself to slow down in life, to think more carefully before speaking or acting.

Alyssa knew she could not bring contentment to John or any man. She was as hollow as this house. John had been right. She had a lot of work to do on the house and herself before either could move forward.

That Thursday afternoon she took sledge hammer in hand behind the staircase and pounded away. Removing crumbling plaster made her feel less hollow. The racket would make her forget about John.

Minutes into her chore, she heard the sander again. She smiled to herself, then groaned at her inability to will John away.

He passed her, saluting as he rolled the sander down the hall and behind the staircase. The hallway led to a suite with a bedroom on either side of a sitting room. Beyond the sitting room was a porch with rusted screens that overlooked Lake Superior in the distance. When done there, John planned to move east of the living room to the large parlor. At the front of the house, the aging boards of the open porch needed attention as well. Upstairs were four more bedrooms. If Alyssa allowed it, John could be kept busy for days just with the floors.

She didn't know much about the history of the farmhouse, only that it'd been empty for years. As she chinked at the plaster that fell from the laths, she imagined all the children that must have tromped up and down the stairs over the years, screaming as they played tag. Alyssa strained to hear her daughter's delightful squeal--

"Nice job!"

Alyssa jumped at John's voice.

"Sorry," he said. "Penny for your thoughts?"

His looks arrested her. She'd pegged him at about her own age of thirty-five, but the deep ridges in his forehead told her life had been harsh to him, too. When he avoided her gaze to bend down and scoop up fallen plaster, she realized John Christopherson also hid behind his passion for work.

"John, what happened to you?"

"I fell off a building. Three stories up."

"I'm sorry."

"It was instant. Painless."

The notion of feeling pain at death had tortured her. John's answer lifted a burden from her.

To avoid the urge to hug him, Alyssa offered, "I can finish cleaning up this plaster. You still have the parlor floor."

John reached out with a thumb to plant a feather touch of electricity on her chin. It brought her body awake in unexpected places. "Whatever you want, Alyssa. That's why I'm here. To do your bidding."

Oh my. Maybe we should've started upstairs in the bedroom.

After he left for the other room, she whacked away at the wall under the stairs. To her shock, plaster gave way in a huge sheet that revealed an open space. There'd been a doorway under the stairwell at one time.

She poked her head into the dark maw. Dust cluttered the floor. She saw an odd lump at the other end of the petite room. Crouching to avoid the low risers overhead, she picked up the object--a palm-sized, red leather pouch, stiff with age.

Back in the hallway, she tipped the pouch upside down. A brooch landed in Alyssa's hand. She gasped. Within a gold rim, six white stones with what looked like diamonds in between formed a ring. Inside that ring, smaller blue gems--the color of Lake Superior on its sunny days--created a circle, too. A green gem the size of Alyssa's thumbnail nestled in the center.

Her hand shook. "John! Help!"

The sander quit.

Once at her side, John whistled. "A secret room with a lovely cache. This bodes well."

"Bodes well for what?" He always made her think in new ways.

"That the party is meant to be and that you're meant to be in this house. Whoever stashed this here knew that an ordinary vagrant or hunter wouldn't be knocking down walls. But they knew somebody who really cared about the place would find it."

Her hand quaked even more. "Who would stash something like this except some jewel thief?" Horror struck her. "They're not coming to the party, are they?"

"I don't know."

"Now what do I do?" Her knees went rubbery. "Obviously there was some disagreement about this brooch or it wouldn't have been hidden behind a secret wall. Somebody must've wanted it and somebody else was making sure they didn't get it. Oh my gosh, maybe there was a murder!"

John plucked the brooch from her hand. "Easy way to find out. You could wear it and see if an aura might appear with answers. It'd look good on you with a little black dress."

She blushed at his teasing. "We have to find the owner."

John flipped the brooch over. "'To Rose, Love Hank'. Know anybody named Rose or Hank?"

Her insides roiled. She knew a Rose, but it made no sense that this would belong to her. "How long do you think this has been behind the stairs?"

"Hard to say. Could be old plaster or newer stuff made to look old. What really matters is that the brooch presented itself and you have to accept that it's your fate to find out about it."

"Not me." She backed off. "You keep it. I don't want some ghost or murdering jewel thief mad at me."

He fingered the brooch. "Would one of your relatives have left this?"

"No. My relatives aren't from around here."

John handed her the brooch then picked up a screw from the plaster. "Looks relatively new. Where are your folks from? When did you last see them?"

Regret settled on her like an itchy sweater. She'd lost holidays with her mother in the past four years. Margaret VanderLune DeClerq loved retelling family stories. She had glass ornaments generations old and each had a story. She'd given two heirloom ornaments to Sadie Rose, one for each Christmas.

It was a tradition now lost. Her mother would eagerly take on the mystery of the brooch. "Both sides of my family were farmers in Door County. But that's on the other side of the state, near Green Bay. My mother still lives there."

"Nobody living around here? What about your father?"

Regret twisted again. "He took off when I was little. I don't know where he ended up. What are you getting at?"

"You know a Rose. Did your father know this Rose, too?"

Her heartbeat sped up with dread. "You think that my father lived in this house? He left this brooch behind? Why? For me to find?"

"County title records should have his name if he were an owner of the property."

"But his name wasn't on the title."

"Did he ever work around here? Maybe he rented the place or camped for free."

Fear bloomed inside Alyssa. "My mother said he was an itinerant worker, always on the move with whatever job he could get. I suppose it's possible he passed through here. But he wasn't rich. He must have stolen this."

"Or not. Take it to the new deputy. If stolen, there'd be reports for insurance purposes."

"Great idea."

She started for the kitchen to get her coat, but John stopped her. "It's dark already. Can't it wait until tomorrow?"

"I can't wait, John. I haven't seen my father in twenty years. What if he really did live here and he knows about this brooch? And he knows about me being here?"

John's face wrinkled. "You don't want to go past the curve at the bottom of the hill."

Flop sweat bathed her entire body. "Why not?"

"You might find me in the car again bleeding to death."

She shivered. "Why would you do that?"

"Research that may prevent the actual accident."

He'd tipped her thinking off-balance again. "So you're play-acting, looking for somebody who may have actually died in a car accident like that?"

"Or who's about to die."

"Can you save them?" Her body hummed with incredulity.

"I don't know, but why else would I be left to wander through the in-between? We all have a purpose. We also have a responsibility to live up to that purpose. Don't we all have to be useful to others?"

John left by walking through the locked kitchen door.

A huge hiss made Alyssa jump aside. Dillinger raced through the closed door. Millicent sat next to her kibble bowl licking a paw, unaffected.

Alyssa stared at the brooch. What did the mysterious array of stones and gems mean? She looked again at the names. Hank. Rose. Did her father really know the same Rose she did? Had her father been lurking nearby at the edges of Alyssa's life, keeping a spying eye on her? Alyssa's throat went dry. She decided she didn't want to know right this minute. She'd heed John's advice and stay put tonight.

She headed for the stairway and bed, but a din of scrapes and loud thunks in the living room stopped her midway on the staircase. "Who's there?"

Alyssa crept back down the stairs. She peeked around the arched doorway, looking to the north where the fireplace puffed a plume of soot.

A diminutive, white-haired woman in a long, black dress, and shoes buttoned over her ankles, dusted herself off. She spat a couple of times. "Heavens to mergatroid, but that's the devil's work, that chimney is, too much for a woman of my age and beauty."

The woman smiled, revealing several missing teeth.

Chapter 3

Alyssa stepped wide-eyed into the room. "Who are you?"

"I am so very sorry to use the chimney, but none of us can walk through your walls. I suspect that's because you're not ready for the party. John mentioned you were a serious case. Look at this place, deary, for shame. We must get to work. I'll thump the rugs."

The woman was rolling up her sleeves.

Alyssa rubbed her temples. *Another dream?* "I suppose I know you somehow?"

"Pshaw, no. I'm your great-great grandmother on your mother's side, Sadie DeForest." *My daughter's namesake.* "I'll be bringing my homemade crackling bread and oxtail soup on Sunday." While swabbing at her sooty face with a dainty handkerchief embroidered in yellow petals around its edges, she squinted at the room. "Oh, deary, where shall we tack up the squirrel tails?"

"Squirrels?" Alyssa was getting queasy again.

"Yes, your Uncle Jay is coming. He's a few uncles back." The woman began gathering up scatter rugs Alyssa hadn't seen before. "His squirrel hunting saved him. Your Uncle Jay Kelly was a horse thief in Ireland. He was hunting the day the constable came for him, but with his weapon he fended off the law and found his way to the boat. I believe that was in 1771. He'll be bringing a dozen fresh, squirming squirrels. After he skins them he always likes to tack the tails up on a wall for good luck. Would the space by that big window do?"

"I guess," Alyssa squeaked, definitely squeamish about squirming squirrels and their tails.

"I advise you hide that brooch in your hand. Your Uncle Jay can't be trusted. It's why he's stuck yet in the in-between."

Alyssa hurried to bed, getting down on her knees to pray for the first time in four years. But at a loss for words, she muttered, "John, get back here and make this go away. I don't want weird dead people in my house. I don't want dead squirrels becoming tapas and wall tapestries!"

When she woke Friday morning, all seemed normal. Millicent snoozed on the bed.

While Alyssa dressed in jeans, a long-sleeved t-shirt and a clean Green Bay Packer sweatshirt, she smiled at the odd dream. A party for dead people? And they'd bring food and squirrel tails?

Glancing about, she failed to see a brooch. She sighed with relief.

Ready to go downstairs to an ordinary day, she glimpsed Lake Superior in the distance through the French doors to the upper deck. She recalled the warm cocoon of John's aura while they'd peered at the lake yesterday--no, in her dream.

She alighted at the foot of the staircase...and spotted the woman with the cloud of white hair dusting in the living room.

Millicent trotted for the kitchen. She didn't even sniff the air. Alyssa groaned. *I'm still inside a damn dream. Wake up! I want my real life back!*

"You need a rabble-rousing, red rooster, young lady. It's almost seven a.m. The coffee should've been put on to boil two hours ago. There will certainly be other relatives coming today to help with preparations."

Alyssa attempted to walk to the kitchen, pretending not to see the woman. But Sadie cackled. Fed up, Alyssa marched over and yanked at her wig. "Trick or treat! Who are you? Tootsie Winters?"

Sadie let out an ear-piercing shriek. "Ouch! My hair!"

Alyssa let go, horrified to find the fluffy, white hair was real. "I'm sorry."

A sparkle on the woman's black dress drew Alyssa closer. "You took the brooch out of my bedroom. You and John are grifters!" The betrayal stung. "You think you can put on a costume because it's Halloween and nobody will notice you robbing them?"

Sadie huffed, "I picked up the brooch when I was dusting. I noticed you have no jewel box. How can a woman exist without a jewel box for her heirlooms that must go to her daughter on her wedding day?"

"I don't have...a daughter. Or heirlooms."

"Well you better get working on both because you're no spring chicken, though with hips like yours you could birth a whole brood until you're forty-five or until consumption takes you."

"You're calling me fat?" Alyssa sniffed the air. "What's that awful smell?"

"Belgian jutte. Cabbage boiled then fried with salt pork. You have a cousin Janet six times removed who needs assistance preparing for the repast and I volunteered to make her jutte ahead of time. It'll work well reheated with the roast boar. That reminds me. Somebody in the in-between asked me where you'd like the fire pit? The pig will need to bake all day tomorrow and into Sunday, especially in cold weather like this."

"We're not cooking a pig over an open fire." *Egads but it sounds like a Christmas song. Where are you, John? I need you!*

Sadie started pushing stuffed chairs around. Alyssa frowned. She'd removed the moth-eaten chairs when she'd moved in. Now they were back, probably dripping bugs. She'd have to fumigate.

Next, with the smell of cabbage stinking up the house, the woman plopped white lacy circles on the chair arms and backs. White circles dressed tables, even the top of an antique pedal pump organ that had somehow materialized.

Sadie said, "These doilies belonged to my mother. They're now yours, handed down through several generations of women. Wasn't she talented? What talent might you have?"

"I--" She'd used to create clay creatures with her daughter. Alyssa focused on the doilies. "I've never seen anything like these in my life."

"I suspect you'll find them in your mother's effects when she dies."

"She's dying soon?" Alyssa panicked.

"I don't think so. When was the last time you talked with her about anything of importance, such as her health?" Sadie shook her head. "Young people. They only think of themselves."

Alyssa bit her lip. What Sadie said held a spark of truth. She and her mother didn't talk of anything of consequence anymore. "Mom and I aren't really doily people."

"Any good funeral needs a doily or two."

"Whose funeral?"

Sadie plunked hands on her hips. "The dead people. Who else has a funeral?"

Alyssa rubbed at her temples. "I thought they were coming for a party?"

"My dear, some will want to bring their caskets. Lying inside a casket helps push the dead spirit to the other side, or at least they hope so."

"We can't have caskets at a party. Whoever heard of such a nutty thing?"

"Alyssa, be respectful of your family. In the 1800s, when they died, their bodies were always on display in the parlor. The minister will be here to say a few words, too. I've warned him he'll have to have a bite of your Great-Grandmother Livingston's blackcap pie or she'll wake the dead."

"We certainly wouldn't want to do that, though waking up sounds mighty good to me." Alyssa did jumping jacks on the spot. "Come on, wake up!"

"Stop that. How do you expect to get a husband when you act so unladylike? Now help me move this small table to the corner. It'll be perfect for those who want to stop for a cup of tea while they view the deceased."

Alyssa lifted a lamp off the table Sadie was shoving. "Who's the dead person trying to die for good?"

"I thought you knew. It's John Christopherson, of course."

Alyssa almost dropped the lamp. "John's leaving for good?"

"He hopes so, though completing the row across the river at these Halloween parties is never a guarantee. He tried two weeks ago by using the casket method, but I think he used poor quality wood. You can't be chintzy. Persimmon is good. Hand-carved oak is always nice." Sadie put a doily on the table. "Isn't he just the nicest man? If anybody deserves a hand-carved--"

"If he passes on, does that mean I'll never see him again?" Alyssa plunked the lamp on the doily.

"That's usually true. It's like crossing the ocean. Most of us only do it once in our lifetime, if at all. In John's case, he wants to pass over desperately. I doubt he'd come back."

"Why can't he stay in the in-between?" *What am I saying? Wake up!*

"I'm sure you've grown close, but you understand. You lost a child. He lost two children in a fire."

The news made Alyssa stagger into a stuffed chair. Dust billowed up.

Sadie patted her shoulder. "Such tragedies fortunately are kind to innocent children. They don't have to earn a spot into Heaven, but they're likely waiting for their father to help them cross the in-between. You can't hold him back from joining his children. He's been working hard to earn passage to help them cross into Heaven."

So John's kindnesses toward Alyssa were earning him his ticket to the afterlife.

She felt foolish, but not betrayed by him after all. She understood the gripping need to see one's children, to hold them, to smell the tops of their heads. She had to tell him she understood, to tell him she was sorry for wanting to hold onto him. "Where's John?"

"I believe he said he was going to a car graveyard somewhere on the other side of Moonstone."

"Probably looking for a wrecked BMW."

Sadie took off the brooch and handed it to Alyssa. "Take this to that fine deputy woman and see who this belongs to."

"But you were wearing it. It must not be real, like..."

Sadie grunted. "Like me? There's only one way to find out. Take it into town and get it looked into, as well as invite real people to the party."

The last thing Alyssa wanted was a real party. Her last party had been the reason she'd rushed through that intersection with her daughter. "No, I can't invite living people."

"John will be disappointed in you."

That put a hitch in her heartbeat. "Why?" Certainly he didn't care. He was leaving her.

"The better the party--the more fun and neighborliness created--the better his chances of passing over. His purpose was to help you, was it not?"

"He said so." Alyssa sighed.

"When friends gather, there's a special power in the room that uplifts us. You want that, don't you?"

She had to want it for John. He needed that boost to rejoin his daughters. But if she helped him do this, he'd be gone. Alyssa was so confused again that she wanted to cry.

"Deary, what does your sweatshirt mean?"

"Green Bay Packers. Football."

"What's a foot ball? Is that like a coming out ball, a cotillion? My sister and I certainly had a gay time at Edith's ball. She married that nice Union soldier who lost his hand..."

Alyssa had to find reality. She skipped breakfast and drove into Moonstone with the brooch.

Deputy Lily Schuster's eyes went agog at the jewels.

Alyssa stammered, "They're real?"

"Give me a moment. They're awfully dusty."

Alyssa sat across from Lily in an office that once was a sundries store for lumberjacks in the 1800s. She couldn't help but notice the lovely sheen on the wood floor. John's handiwork? "Who refinished the floor?"

"A teenager from over at Port Cliff. He unfortunately got into trouble with rat poison in a pie that caused a lady's death, so I'm without anybody to finish the work here."

"How horrible."

"It was a tragic accident. He's in therapy."

"What about the brooch? Can you trace it?"

"Something worth this much was likely reported missing sometime."

Alyssa leaned forward with excitement. "How much do you think it's worth?"

"Easily a quarter of a million or so."

Alyssa blinked. "That much?"

"My friend Kirsten VanBrocklin is something of an expert on jewels. Why not have her take a look?"

"Where would I find her?"

"She's the chef at The Jingle Bell Inn. I'm sure she's there today, what with the party in the school gym for the kids tomorrow night before Halloween day. She's catering."

Alyssa didn't want to be inside a restaurant kitchen. It would bring back unwanted memories. But she thought about how hard John was working to rejoin his daughters. He needed her help.

"Deputy..."

"Lily is fine among us girls."

The casualness of "girls" reminded Alyssa of Sadie's words. *"Friendship uplifts people. Invite living people to the party."* "Lily, I'm having a party on Sunday. Would you come?"

"I'd love to."

"It's dish-to-pass." She expected the deputy to back out.

Instead, Lily clapped her hands. "Wait until you try my skubanky." She smiled at Alyssa's odd look. "Comes from my fiancé's mother. She's Czechoslovakian. Before I met her about the only thing domestic I knew how to do was iron. I love to iron. You?"

"Not really." Wrinkled clothes were on their own.

"You mix mashed potatoes with flour, roll them into hotdog shapes, fry them in lots of fat until brown, serve with maple syrup. You'll love my spanking skubankies!"

Enjoying the deputy's enthusiasm, Alyssa said, "I'll fast all day tomorrow so I can pig out on them on Sunday." But she sobered, embarrassed to ask the next question. "Who else might I invite? I don't know anybody."

"Marge at the IGA would love an invitation. She's a new woman since getting engaged to Tony. You know how voluptuous in size she is. The story goes that she wore a bikini in public last summer and Tony fell in love. He was the chef on Kirsten's husband's yacht. Still is, though they sold the yacht."

Alyssa's head spun. "Does this getting to know my neighbors get any easier?"

"Not in Moonstone. Here. Use paper." Lily handed her a pen and paper before continuing. "And ask Tom and Lily Bauer. She's a teller at the bank."

"Two Lilys in town. That's lovely."

"We can try for other flower names." Lily looked at the back of the brooch. "How about we start by finding a Rose?"

Alyssa paled. She focused her gaze downward on the list. "Who else should I invite?"

"Of course Tootsie Winters. She'd love bringing women to town with flower names as a publicity stunt. Talk to her about the idea at your party."

"I'd rather not. She sounds a bit intense."

"She is. Tootsie and her husband, Bob, run the honeymoon cruises. They bought Kirsten's and Jonathon's yacht. Also invite Peter and Crystal. Don't forget old Henri and his twenty-something girlfriend, Felicity Starr. They've lasted two months already so it's best to invite them because everybody would talk about them anyway." Lily laughed.

Alyssa decided that being neighborly meant putting up with a lot of quirks. She stuck with it, though. She wanted real people at her house, not dead people.

Lily added, "And don't forget Claire Lone Eagle and her husband. They've had a real bad time of things lately, what with John in a coma."

Alyssa snapped her head up. "John who?"

"John Christopherson. He and Claire's husband were working construction down in New Orleans a month ago when he fell off a mansion roof they were repairing."

There's a real John Christopherson. He's not just part of my dreams. "He's going to be okay?"

Lily's fair complexion faded paler. "He broke a lot of bones, has a bunch of internal injuries, I hear. Don't tell Claire this, because she's always worried about her husband, too, but I don't think John's going to make it."

Alyssa clutched the pen in her hand so hard she broke a fingernail. "Do you know what hospital he's in?"

"No, but I could find out. It's likely not New Orleans. Since Katrina they've taken patients all over the United States. But give me a little time. I don't want to call Claire or her husband. They're so distraught they can't even talk at the mention of John's name."

Alyssa recalled how Claire always seemed to be on the go at the casino with no time for chatting. "Sure. Thank you. But call me as soon as you know anything."

Chapter 4

With each step across Moonstone's square, Alyssa experienced different emotions: elation over there being a real John; anger over his wish to pass over; selfishness for wanting him despite his children needing him; sadness over being unable to help him.

But how could she know this John without having met him for real? Alyssa felt as if she'd fallen into a deep crack in the earth, been digested by monsters, then spit up with a sixth sense.

But that couldn't be. She must have read about John in a newspaper and forgotten.

When Alyssa searched her pocket for a tissue, she came up with a white handkerchief crotcheted with yellow rosebuds. *Sadie's?* Real or not, the hankie was perfect for sopping up tears.

Presentable again, she crossed the street to enter The Jingle Bell Inn. Patrons filled the mansion's dining room overlooking a sweeping lawn and Lake Superior. Alyssa's mouth watered at the smell of fried eggs and omelets, buttery pancakes with maple syrup, hash browns and bacon.

She checked her cell phone. *Lily, please call. I must know about John.*

A blonde woman in a chef's hat peeked out from the kitchen then hurried over. Kirsten Peplinski VanBrocklin said, "Sorry to keep you waiting. Coffee and a stack of cranberry pancakes are on me."

The graciousness relaxed Alyssa. She held out the brooch. "Lily Schuster said you might know what this is worth."

"Moonstones!" Kirsten laughed so hard her white hat tipped back. "My husband gave me a dozen moonstones when he kidnapped me on his boat. They were gifts for my bridesmaids."

"He knew he wanted to marry you the first time you met?"

"Oh yeah. And it was his way to force me to find new friends around here. Men like him are rare."

They're like John.

Kirsten examined the moonstones. "Blue veins, hint of man-in-the-moon faces--the more valuable kind."

"My carpenter and I found the brooch in the farmhouse that I'm refurbishing."

Kirsten's smile brightened. "I desperately need a carpenter. I don't think the enclosed aviary's going to be done by Christmas for the wedding. Send your guy my way."

If only. "I heard him say he had another gig right after my house."

"Too bad." Kirsten sized up the brooch. "I have a magnifying glass in the kitchen."

In the stainless steel haven, steam rose from pans and pots. The soft heat on her skin gave Alyssa pause. She expected John to be standing beside her. But he wasn't.

While Kirsten searched a desk covered with cookbooks, Alyssa asked, "Would you like to come to my dish-to-pass Halloween party?"

"I'd love to. I have a recipe for mushrooms stuffed with wild rice, cranberry raisins and cheddar cheese that I'm dying to try on people."

"Sounds perfect."

"I'm still trying to figure out how to turn my garlic mashed potatoes into finger food."

"Lily's bringing a potato thing already."

"Her skubanky from Marcus's mom. I want to steal that recipe and she won't let me."

"Make your own version."

"Nah. Feels odd to steal from a law officer."

Alyssa grinned at Kirsten's visible shudder.

Kirsten finally found her magnifying glass. "What do you do?"

"I'm a card dealer at the casino."

"With this there's no need to go to any casino. Easily a half-million."

"What?!"

"My husband deals in fine jewels for his rich clients. This is the real deal. Moonstones, diamonds, and sapphires of the highest grade. And the emerald--wow." Lily flipped the brooch over. "Who are Hank and Rose? These stones are known for love and devotion--deep faith in another person. If you remember, Prince Charles re-started the sapphire craze for engagements when he gave one to Princess Diana."

Alyssa decided to trust Lily. Chefs knew how to be discreet with recipes and gossip overheard in their restaurants. "I once knew a Rose. A waitress that I met in Duluth a few years ago. She was kind to me when I needed it. I named my daughter for her. Sadie Rose."

"How lovely. But no Hanks?"

"Fresh out of Hanks."

"The closest we have to that around here is Henri LeBarron. But he's in his eighties and goes strictly by Henri."

A dead end. Alyssa recalled John's questions about possible past owners. "Where might I find somebody who knows area history?"

"Tootsie Winters knows everything or at least thinks she does. She lives a few miles out. Just follow the signs for the lavender chickens and the giant prehistoric beaver."

Alyssa grimaced. The Moonstone area was one surprising adventure after another.

Tootsie lived in a yellow house next to a marsh and thick timber. A wolf-proof, enclosed yard by a shed contained oddly colored, fluffy chickens pecking about. And then there was Tootsie.

A fleshy woman with short, silver hair, she wore a flamingo pink fleece leisure outfit with strawberries appliquéd across the bosom and down the sleeves. She greeted Alyssa with Lulu, a lavender-hued chicken, in her arms. Lulu went with them up into Tootsie's packed attic where she kept old township records. "I'm sure we'll find something." She handed Lulu to Alyssa, who sneezed at the ticklish, ostrich-like feathers. Lulu warbled before nose-diving into sleep in the crook of Alyssa's arm.

Tootsie popped up from a wooden chest waving an old newspaper. "Here's a start."

Dated 1995, the local shopper paper had an article about area haunted houses. Alyssa exchanged Lulu for the paper.

"So it's true my farmhouse has always been haunted?"

"At least abandoned off and on for twenty years. Of course, being haunted may be why the owners abandoned it. They didn't want to be part of an underground railroad for lost souls."

"What's that?"

"An underground railroad is what they called the secret homes and people who helped the slaves escape to freedom in the 1800s. Some houses, especially big ones high on a hill, act as the same thing for spirits in the in-between."

"You make it sound like I'm running a B&B for dead people."

"You might be. They like to party before they pass over and go on up." The pink woman set her lavender chicken aside on a dusty rocking chair before bending over to root about in another box. "Have you seen any ghosts? I'd give anything to see one."

Alyssa stared gape-mouthed at the woman--or more accurately, her big pink butt. "If I say I've seen something it makes me nuts, right?"

"You have seen ghosts! I'm jealous."

Alyssa clung to the newspaper. "I hear noises is all. A brick fell from my fireplace, but if you saw the condition of my--"

"Who came down the chimney?"

"Nobody."

"Hah! Somebody did. I can see it in the twinkle of your eyes."

"How can you know that somebody came down my chimney?"

"I know."

She knew. As Alyssa knew things for certain.

Tootsie plunked her heft down on the wood chest. "Don't tell anybody, but I hear voices. I see things, too, except for ghosts or spirits, darn it all. People think I'm crazy, but I can see events before they happen and know they'll be a success. Right now I've been seeing all of Moonstone planted with moon flowers that open at midnight, with throngs of tourists coming for rides in white carriages pulled by white horses. What do you think?"

Alyssa swallowed hard. "Dreamer or seer, you're a person with magical ideas. I love the idea of Moonstone at midnight. I'll even help."

Tootsie hooted. Her strawberries bounced up and down. "There're two of us who can see things, who can 'just know'. Not even my husband knows about this. He thinks my craziness is menopause. You'll keep it a secret?"

This commonality with Moonstone's resident kook would take a while to digest. "You have my word, Tootsie."

Tootsie went head-first into more boxes. "I heard some fella lived in your house for a year or two not so long ago, maybe four years ago, then again recently, but I never saw the guy."

Could Alyssa's father truly be spying on her? "How old was he?"

"Not sure. I could find out."

"Thanks." Alyssa scanned the newspaper for any mention of a DeClerq. "All it says is that hunters used the place in bad weather."

"And homeless people, teenagers, and probably those scumbags trying to create meth."

"Drugs?"

"It's likely. Lily's been having a heck of a time tracking down the labs. They started to creep in here twenty years ago. Lily needs help, but there's no budget. The best thing to happen for her and that old farmhouse is you living there to keep the creeps out."

Alyssa got a chill. If John was right about her father passing through here, could her father have been involved with drugs? Was that why he left her and her mother two decades ago? For a fast, illegal buck?

"Tootsie, can I keep this?"

"Sure. I'll keep looking through these trunks. I'll let you know right away what I find."

"If you also find anything about jewel heists, would you save those stories, too?"

Tootsie went bug-eyed with excitement. "Do we have a Butch and Sundance in our midst? Capone visited the North Woods, but that's southeast of here. By golly, Moonstone could use a good legend to bring in tourists. The giant beaver found in my yard by Professor Landen hasn't been enough."

"I'm having a party on Sunday for my neighbors. Would you and your husband like to come?"

"I'll bring deviled eggs!"

"Perfect for Halloween."

"Can I bring Lulu?"

"I have a cat." *Maybe two.*

"Not wise then. Lulu's quite the watch-hen. Very protective. I'd hate to see her chasing your poor cat around the house. You really should think of getting better protection, like a chicken that can make a fuss. Living all alone out in the woods is dangerous. People could walk into your house at any moment of the day and night."

Indeed.

When she got home Friday afternoon, Alyssa didn't find John. Had he died? She was so distraught she called the casino to beg off working that night. Finishing her kitchen floor was all she could manage with her mind scrambled with so many worries: her daughter, the brooch, "Rose", her missing father, and now Tootsie Winters spooking her. And she had to contend with more dead relatives about in the living room.

Sadie had been joined by Joette--Alyssa's mother's aunt who had died in the 1970s from breast cancer, and her daughter, Moonbeam--a nurse who died in the 1990's Gulf War. Joette and Moonbeam sang Beatles songs over the high-pitched whine of Joette's canister vacuum. Moonbeam had hauled in beanbag chairs and lava lamps while Sadie shook out antique rag rugs.

When the women began the soulful song, "Yesterday", Alyssa slumped on the cold kitchen floor in tears. The song got her every time.

A tap on her shoulder made her look up. "John!"

She launched to her feet ready to fling herself into his arms, her heart bursting toward him, but Dillinger hissed at her as he trotted by, which made her step farther back from her foolishness. The cat was wet and matted. John was, too, with leaves stuck in his mussed black hair.

"What happened?" She reached for a towel to give John. It taunted her that he used it--as if he were real.

"I decided to follow the creek to see if the guy from the car had followed it, too, after the accident. We slipped while trying to cross the creek. But I suppose that was good practice for us."

She couldn't take his flippancy. "John, where are you?"

"Right here."

"I mean your body. Where is it?"

"I don't know."

"Why not?"

"The past doesn't always stay with you when we're like this. The past doesn't matter sometimes. My body doesn't matter anyway. I'm here to help you with the dish-to-pass party."

She grabbed her phone off the counter and shook it to make sure it was working. "I'm going to find your body, don't worry. I'll help put you back together."

"But I might be like Humpty Dumpty. You have to face that."

His serious look weighed her with sadness.

Dillinger plunked his butt near the refrigerator and started licking his privates. Alyssa was grateful for the distraction. "Can't you teach that beast any manners?"

"I've tried. He doesn't listen to me for some reason. Why are you so nervous? You've invited live people, haven't you?" John's smile marched all the way up to the twinkle in his chocolate-colored eyes.

"Yeah. A bunch of people I don't know." She ached to kiss him. "I also found out this place is haunted."

"Duh."

He always made her smile when she most needed it. "According to what I read, there were several past owners of parcels of land here that were once tied together in one big tract of logging timber."

He picked up his one-eyed cat to dry him off. "What if your father owned a parcel? What if the brooch was part of some payment for land?" His eyes grew dark as the morning coffee still in its pot on the counter. "Or did he die near here?"

She hadn't expected that information. "Have you met him recently in your wanderings?"

He tossed the towel over to the sink. "Not yet in the in-between. But that doesn't mean he hasn't died."

The possible loss gnawed at her. Why did she even care if he were alive yet? She forced herself back to the green tiles on the floor.

John joined her, brushing down paste in front of her. "Are you afraid of him showing up on Sunday?"

"Dead or alive, yes."

"Why?"

Her hands shook as she laid a green tile in place. "Because of the pain he's caused me and my mom by disappearing. It makes me want to spit on his shoes."

"But you can't really do that because you love him and he loves you."

"I doubt it."

"Alyssa, you're loveable. Trust me. There's got to be a good reason he left. I bet he smiles when he thinks of you. Your little girl smiles when she talks about you."

"I thought you said she was sad?" Alyssa sat back on the floor.

He kept on laying tiles for her. "She's repeated a couple of times that it wasn't your fault."

Alyssa could barely muster a whisper. "I speeded up to get through a yellow light. My car rolled on impact and Sadie Rose's car seat came apart." She choked. "Apparently, in my hurry I hadn't buckled it properly."

When he reached over to touch her cheek, she wanted to sink into him, to tell him the rest of it. But it wouldn't be fair to him. To reveal who else had been harmed by her careless actions would only burden him. John didn't need her grief piled on his own. He needed strength to move on.

He said, "You may have gone through a yellow light, but it wasn't red. That means the other driver ran through a red one. What happened to him or her?"

"A bunch of teenagers broadsided me but their airbags went off and they walked away from it all."

"Were they charged in court?"

"No. The driver's insurer put a price on my daughter, though. She was worth two-hundred-fifty thousand dollars." She swallowed a sob.

"Alyssa, listen to me. The car seat was defective and the teenagers made a horrible mistake. Of course you got paid a pile of money. It's not what your daughter was worth. And none of it was your fault."

"But I can't seem to get past it. I didn't need to be in such a hurry."

She barely had her handkerchief out of her pocket when John gathered Alyssa in his arms. Being with him was like settling on a hearth next to an oak log fire. She'd miss him. Already she ached for him. "You won't leave me before the party, will you?"

"Cross over before this dish-to-pass party?" He laughed while taking the hankie to dry off her cheeks. "I haven't had a decent meal in ages."

Because you're lying in some hospital on an IV drip, a liquid diet.

She forced a smile. "We've got a ton of work tomorrow before Sunday comes. Could you paint the parlor for me now?"

"I'd rather sand the floors. I was getting the hang of that." He winked. "But then I'm good at hanging upside down in cars, too."

"I'd rather you not do any more of that."

"I'll try."

"Thanks, John. Thanks for being a friend when I needed one most. I wish you could stay."

"I'll try to stay until you find out about the brooch's owner. I'm curious, too."

He left her to go find the paint. Dillinger trotted after him. Millicent as usual paid them no heed.

How can that brooch with its inscription matter to John? Why can't he stay for me? Why can't I be his raison d'etre?

She picked up her cell phone, pressing Lily's number. "Have you found out anything?"

"It seems he was moved recently for some reason. I'll get you the right phone numbers to call."

Alyssa had hope. "Where is he?"

"A Texas hospital."

So far away. And she had her party in only a day and a half. She sagged. But he was alive. Hope put a smile on her face and a lightness in her walk. She even waved goodnight to Sadie on her way up the stairs to bed.

Chapter 5

On Saturday morning Alyssa felt upbeat for the first time in years. It helped to work alongside John repairing the alcove. She reveled in doing ordinary things with him. Few words were necessary. Instead, comfort hummed from the mere companionship and teamwork, the inadvertent touch of their shoulders or marrying of hands while putting a board in place. She had never worked like this with her ex. He'd always had his own way of doing things, but then, so had she. They painted the alcove in a cheery apple red hue, and found a table in the barn that would turn the space into a punch station.

Disaster struck after lunch when Sadie began hanging pictures of dead relatives. "Deary, no home should be without a peek at who gave you your cheekbones, ears, toes, and twinkle."

Alyssa was making cowboy cookies with orange M&M's in the kitchen when Sadie insisted she "come see".

A mishmash of photos and tintypes in gilded frames covered the flocked wall between the living room and parlor. Sadie said, "We're missing an important one. Your daughter."

The good feelings drained from Alyssa. "I don't want my daughter paraded about like that on Halloween."

Sadie sank into a chair, her face crumpling into her fancy hankie. John scowled at Alyssa from a ladder in the parlor. He was hanging an antique chandelier. "That's exactly what you need. To share Sadie Rose."

An ache ripped through her. "I can't. You understand. You lost two children. I don't want to have to talk about Sadie Rose with every person who walks through my doors--or walls--tomorrow."

He came to her with his billfold flipped open. "I show them off to everybody."

His daughters looked about ten and twelve, with John's black hair and his twinkling, brown eyes. The girls sat on a board fence with a dapple gray horse behind them.

If only Sadie Rose had lived. "They liked to ride?"

"They loved Buster."

"What became of Buster?"

"My ex-wife took him, which is good. He's well cared for."

Alyssa swallowed. She hadn't even considered whether John was still married or not. She had rushed ahead into needing him without thinking of John's feelings. She looked around. Sadie, Joette and Moonbeam had disappeared. "Do you want to tell me about it?"

A shadow doused the light in his eyes. "The fire was an accident. A candle in their bedroom fell over. We didn't know they'd lit one after we'd gone to bed. They'd also dismantled their smoke alarm. We carried them out, both of us sustaining burns, but our children died of smoke inhalation. My wife never recovered from the emptiness."

"That's what it is, John. Emptiness."

"But people aren't meant to remain empty. We're vessels who need filling. I wanted more children. My wife didn't. But looking at this photo makes me know exactly what I need. If I can't have real children, then it's time to go see these cute little buggers."

He was smiling at her. Alyssa's heart swelled toward him.

He said, "Try it. Put the photo on the wall. It'll start filling you with a new feeling you didn't expect. We'll all get to see where Sadie Rose got her ears, nose, and twinkle."

Sadness overwhelmed Alyssa. There was so much she could never tell John. "All little kids have a twinkle in their eyes."

"A lesson for all of us. We adults should make it our job to give each other a twinkle." He winked at her. "There. I just blew you a twinkle. It looks nice on you. You should wear one in those big brown eyes more often."

Alyssa's sadness lifted with that.

John took the photo of his children and taped it on her wall. "Put Sadie Rose's picture up beside them and she won't be alone. We'll both have our children at the party."

Alyssa imagined crawling into one of those dreams where her daughter was so real she could smell her sweet, baby-powdered skin.

She fetched the photo of her daughter dressed in a pink fairy Halloween costume. She hesitated, but John's reassuring nod helped her find the strength to put her precious pink fairy up on the wall with the rest of her family and John's children.

The photo wall took her breath away. The twinkle in her daughter's eyes was repeated in several others' eyes. A lump formed in her throat. Her daughter's presence had created magic. The stirrings of completeness came to Alyssa. She looked at the wall of photos, the girls in particular, then looked at John, finally realizing what was happening to her. She was re-awakening to what it meant to be part of a family. Her vessel, for at least this moment, felt full.

"Thanks, John."

"It's what I'm here for," he said, before going outside to repair boards on the front steps.

On Sunday at exactly three p.m., with slate clouds spitting snow, dead relatives walked through walls carrying food from their era and culture. A Belgian pioneer from Door County brought wicker baskets of blood sausage and small crocks of fresh, hot fried cabbage. A German relative arrived with knofli noodles topped with strips of goat cheese.

Joette brought true American cuisine, a tater-tot casserole. Moonbeam arrived with macaroni and cheese with catsup as garnish. Alyssa's mother's deceased aunt from the 1960s brought a lime gelatin ring with carrots and celery chopped inside. She'd put dollops of mayonnaise on top, with more mayo lathered around the perimeter of the wiggly green concoction.

Alyssa's Uncle Jay--twinkly mischievous eyes--brought a sack of dead squirrels. He passed through the kitchen wall to the outdoors to skin them. Others from the 1700s and 1800s brought freshly shot fowl and a wild boar, which somebody mentioned was roasting in a pit somewhere in Alyssa's yard.

Relatives from the 1940s and '50s brought coconut and German chocolate cakes four layers tall. They proudly told Alyssa their secret-- toothpicks. She smiled because she remembered her mother showing her the same trick when she was a little girl.

One relative in his Union blue uniform brought salt-water pickles, of all things. Alyssa noted he was missing a hand.

Uncle Jay's first wife in the Americas, Betsy, brought homemade root beer, concocted from hops, roots of burdock, yellow dock, sarsaparilla and spikenard.

Alyssa exchanged a look with John across the crowded living room. He winked at her. She winked back.

She rushed about finding space for all the dishes-to-pass, some with hand-carved wood ladles and gourd dippers.

Kirsten arrived with her stuffed mushrooms and tombstone cupcakes with red syrup blood drizzled over the top. Alyssa assumed Kirsten wouldn't be able to see, smell, or taste any of the dishes-to-pass from her dead relatives, yet the chef bounded in as if she'd landed in nirvana. "You cooked! Didn't you sleep?"

"I didn't, I did, I'm not sure." Alyssa closed the front door.

Kirsten had already dipped a fork into the succotash. "How quaint! A Pilgrim dish. How ever did you think to make this?"

"Oh," she said, taking in the crowded room of motley relatives, including her Uncle Jay tacking fuzzy rodent tails on the front wall, "I was in the mood for squirrel, corned beef, and turnips."

"Let me at your card file. Flash me the succotash."

"I..." In all her years of cooking Alyssa had never thought of writing down the recipes of her relatives, including her own mother. An oversight to be corrected. "I'll see what I can do."

Tootsie and Bob Winters knocked next on the front door. Tootsie, dressed in a shocking pink princess outfit not unlike the photo of Alyssa's daughter, proudly handed her a big bowl of something she called "Spit-Up Casserole".

"What's in it?"

"Spam, spaghetti, mayo, Velveeta cheese cubes melted, and broccoli to cancel out the fat. I melt the cheese with a little Seven-Up, thus the name."

"I love Spit-Up Casserole already, Tootsie. The perfect side dish for squirrel succotash."

As Tootsie and Bob found a spot for the gut-bomb dish, Kirsten came up to Alyssa screaming, "You have mulgipuder, reeble, and abenkater!"

"I do?"

"Thank goodness you created the cards with historical notes for each dish-to-pass."

"I did?"

"I love Halloween. It's fun to think about how our relatives might be partying up in the sky. What do you think your relatives are doing?"

Uncle Jay was helping other men haul in the whole, roasted boar, its skin mahogany color. "Oh, I suspect they're bobbing for apples."

"Where should I put this caramel apple pie?" asked Kirsten. "On the casket?"

Casket?! Following the men with the boar, a mix of dead men relatives and real neighbors hefted an ornate, wood casket through the front door and the living room, finally resting it in place on a sturdy frame in the parlor.

This can't be. Alyssa remembered what Grandma Sadie had said about needing a fancy casket to help one pass over.

When the men left the parlor, Alyssa wound through the crowd in the living room to get to the casket. "John, where are you?"

A draft fluttered Alyssa's hair. Grandma Sadie stood at her side. "Deary, we miss him, too."

Alyssa trembled. "He can't be dead yet. He promised."

Kirsten asked, "Who's dead?"

The dead people rearranged the furniture to give the casket space. They put dishes-to-pass about the room. A couple of women in long dresses brought pitchers of lemonade to side tables.

Alyssa didn't see a preacher. Good. They couldn't perform a funeral service yet. She must have time. To do what? She had to save John, but how? She refused to let him die right here in her parlor. He said he'd wait until she resolved the mystery of the brooch.

Kirsten peered at her with a quirky grin. "Relax. It's going well. Even Tootsie's impressed. I can't figure out why she hasn't dissed you as she's always done with everybody who's new to the Moonstone community."

"So you really don't see anything out of place?"

"This is the most fabulous party I've ever attended. I still can't believe you roasted a whole pig."

"Neither can I." Alyssa tested her. "Did you check out the blood sausage?"

"It's half gone already. Where do you find that delicacy?"

She lied. "My mother sent it from Door County."

Kirsten rushed off to serve punch. Alyssa searched frantically for John. He needed to know the whole truth about Sadie Rose. It must be her fault he was eager to pass over. Had he sensed that she'd held back a lot of things from him? That he couldn't trust Alyssa?

She went to the photo of her pink princess. "Please help me find John."

"They're darling." A tall woman with long, auburn hair stood beside Alyssa. "I'm Crystal Hagan. My farm is a couple of miles as the crow flies from yours. I teach first grade."

The grade Sadie Rose would be in had she lived. "Have you seen a tall man with black, wavy hair and brown eyes that twinkle?"

Crystal wrapped an arm around the man beside her. "Sounds yummy, but I've already caught my man. This is my fiancé, Peter LeBarron."

Alyssa's heart lurched at how handsome he was because he reminded her of John, but a generation older. "You're getting married at Christmas."

"We hope," he said. "We thought it'd be last summer, then that got changed with the horrible pie contest death. Now nothing's coming together with our additions to the North Pole. I want the setting to look just right for my lovely bride."

He kissed Crystal in a way that made Alyssa long for John even more. The yearning scared the heck out of her. She didn't want to be an empty vessel anymore.

When the Santa Claus-like Henri LeBarron came in, assisted by his young, drop-dead gorgeous girlfriend, Felicity Starr, Kirsten nudged Alyssa. "You two could be sisters."

Felicity laughed. "I used to be a sister. A nun, that is."

Henri eased into a chair. "There's been nothing nun-like about you, Felix."

She wrapped her arms around him and kissed his rosy cheeks. "Shall I tell them?"

"Don't see why not," he said. "Half the town's here. Might as well control our own gossip."

"We're having a baby! If it's a girl, we're naming her Rose. If it's a boy, well, we don't know yet!"

Henri pulled Felicity into his lap.

While the crowd clapped, Alyssa turned away in shock. *Rose? The name on the back of the brooch is Rose.*

Sadie's face soured. "She's with child and they're not married? The old coot should be horse-whipped."

Henri toasted with a cup of punch. "I would be honored if my daughter could have all of Moonstone's women as her godmothers. That includes our newest addition, Alyssa Swain."

This was awful. Worse than awful. Everybody was clapping for Alyssa, even the dead relatives and her grandmother.

Alyssa whispered to Grandma Sadie, "How can you be unhappy that they're having a baby but happy that I'm a godmother for that baby?"

"Didn't you hear? They're naming her Rose. Like your daughter."

Alyssa noticed Grandma Sadie was wearing the brooch again. Did that mean it wasn't real, that it belonged to a Rose in the afterlife? "Is my Rose getting ready to come back as--?"

"Their Rose? No. That's not how it works. But she may be the one to find your godchild a guardian angel. That is, if your daughter is allowed to cross over. You can't find angels if you're not in Heaven yet."

"What do you mean by 'allowed'?"

"She wouldn't be hesitating to cross over unless something in her real life wasn't returned to rights yet. Perhaps she's waiting for John to finish putting things to right, and then he'll help her across."

Alyssa shivered. "No, it's me, Grandma." She had to figure out how to help John and Sadie Rose. "Can I have the brooch?"

Sadie fingered the gems. "For what purpose? It's a keepsake. You have no children to hand it down to."

"Thanks for the reminder." Alyssa took back the brooch. "It says 'To Rose, Love Hank'. Is Felicity's baby the Rose on this brooch? Can you see the future?"

Sadie frowned. "All things are possible. The brooch is passing between our worlds and timelines now. If the Rose on this brooch is Felicity's baby, that means you need to find a Hank and give this back to him. He has to have it if he's ever going to give it to Rose someday. And, deary, I advise you must do this by midnight because after Halloween is done most of us will likely disappear for a year and the brooch might go with us."

"Crap." She had to find a "Hank"? On Halloween? "Double crap."

"Watch your mouth. I said the S-word after learning my husband had an affair. That's why I'm still in the in-between."

"Sadie, do this one good deed and maybe you'll cross over. Give me a sign that the brooch is okay to claim it as my own, that it wasn't stolen by my father or part of some drug deal."

The brooch fell to the floor with a clatter. That was a sign? Alyssa slipped it into her pocket.

Sadie had disappeared. A dirge in the parlor caught Alyssa's attention.

She bolted to the casket and lifted the lid. "John?" She didn't find a body. Her heart sprouted wings. But where was he? She knew. He was tenacious about saving the person in the BMW.

After grabbing her yellow barn coat, Alyssa fought her way outside through spits of sleet and snow, got in her Jeep, then sailed down Porcupine Hill.

"John!"

He was hanging upside down in the car, blood dripping off his jaw.

"John, get out of there."

"I can't."

"You have to. It's your turn to have faith in me. You have to stop these death-defying things, like working on mansion roofs without ropes. I'm going to make things right with Rose. I'm going to return things to their original condition. It could be that the BMW crash is related. That's why it happened here. I was supposed to find you."

"I told you your little Rose is fine."

"Not that Rose. The waitress I knew."

Sleet pricked like knives at her. She crouched down to touch his face but felt nothing, which frightened her. "John, I have to hurry. Hang in there."

"Very funny."

"I didn't mean it that way."

It was crazy to abandon her own party, but Alyssa suspected they'd be too busy talking about babies, weddings, and squirrel tails to notice.

With roads getting progressively icier as she headed west, it took her over an hour to get to Duluth, and then another half hour to find the Fuel & Food Truck Stop on the west edge of the city.

The interior bright lights of the diner blinded her. The place had a black-checkered floor dirtied by snow slush, auto racing posters, and a jukebox playing a plaintive love song. Alyssa spotted Rose Davenport at a long counter where truckers hunkered over coffee or a cheap meal.

Her nerves on fire, Alyssa made her way to the counter. Rose didn't recognize her. She poured coffee like a robot. Despite being twenty, the woman with "Rose" on the nametag had dark circles under her eyes and looked as worn as the slouching truckers. Her waist-length, blonde hair was tucked haphazardly behind her ears. She wore no jewelry, no wedding ring. But she was very pregnant.

Compassion burst inside Alyssa. "Rose? It's me. Alyssa Swain. Your daughter's mother."

Chapter 6

Ya cut yer hair."

Rose's simple greeting after four years helped Alyssa keep her courage. "Yes, well, after the funeral I couldn't be bothered with taking care of hair."

"Me, too. Haven't cut mine or curled it since then. Want some of that pumpkin pie there?"

"Sure." Alyssa sipped the hot, black coffee. "You're having a baby."

"Suppose." Rose served the pie. "Want whipped cream? We got real Cool Whip."

"No, thanks." She couldn't touch the pie.

Rose went to refill a coffee cup and came back.

Alyssa asked, "Are you getting married?"

"Not sure, but I'm keepin' it, no matter what David does."

David. Not Hank. "What does David do? How'd you meet?"

"At the tech school. We got our GEDs. He's a welder at a body shop."

"But there's something wrong? You don't love each other?"

Rose shrugged it off.

Alyssa flinched. This couple had to get back together or disaster could happen. She knew. She fingered the brooch in her jeans' pocket, mulling. "What do you mean 'no matter what David does'?"

"He wants to start his own auto body shop. Wants to move away from the city."

"What's wrong with that?"

"We don't have money. That's why we're not married. He says he wants to find a place first. But a business costs money. We'll be stuck somewhere with nothing and a baby. I'd rather keep on livin' with my mom."

Who Alyssa remembered had been divorced twice and worked as little as possible. Alyssa could see the essence of a lost dream in Rose's dull eyes that once were sparkling at sixteen. Rose had resigned herself to a life she didn't deserve. But the welder boyfriend had a dream. If he got his dream, Rose might have her dream, too. Alyssa recalled the young woman was quite the artist in high school and had wanted to create her own comic strip, to make people laugh.

Alyssa asked, "Do you know what your baby is? A boy?"

"A girl."

This wasn't working out at all. If Henri and Felicity were having a girl, then this woman had to have a boy to make destiny work out for everybody. "The doctor said so?"

"No. But mom says it's the way I'm carrying the baby."

The unreliable mom said that? Alyssa grinned. "If it's a girl, what're you going to name her?"

"Petunia."

Think quick. "You're so beautiful and your name is beautiful. Maybe our baby Rose wouldn't mind if you named your baby Rose after her big sister."

A smile spread on the girl's face for the first time. "That's sweeter 'n' pie."

Close call. But there was still this thing with Felicity and Henri being sure they were having a girl. "What if it's a boy?"

A snapping energy erupted in Rose's blue eyes. "After my grandpa. He always remembered my birthday, always bought a cake, and when I was little having a store-bought cake was tits."

"What's your grandpa's name?"

"Hank."

Alyssa wanted to dance about the diner. Instead, she laid her hand over the young woman's hand. "Rose, everything's going to be all right for you and David. I promise." *Some day, your little boy is going to marry a very, very rich little girl. But for now...*

Alyssa took out the brooch and laid it on the counter. "This is yours."

"Holy smokes!"

"Somebody gave it to me, but it won't really do me much good." She turned it over for Rose to read.

"To Rose, Love Hank." Rose's mouth twitched. "You're spooking me out."

"It's Halloween, after all."

"So if I have a Hank, how does he find this little Rose?"

"I'm betting if you sold off some of the emeralds, sapphires, and diamonds in that brooch that you and David can marry, start your own business in some other place, even buy a house. But keep all the moonstones. They might give David a hint of where to start his business. Maybe your son will meet some nice girl in this new community. He can give her that brooch--with colored crystals to fill in where the gems once were--with a great family story attached."

Tears shimmered in Rose's eyes as she touched the gems. "We can start our life for real? Are you sure you want to do this?"

"I'm very sure, Rose. I'm sorry I haven't stayed in touch. That was wrong. You gave me the best years of my life. You deserve a magical life."

"So do you, Mrs. Swain. You were a good mother. You'll be one again. I know it. If that's what you want."

It was a question. Alyssa's heart pounded harder than ever. "I need to get a husband first."

Alyssa fought her way through the snowy evening back to the bottom of Porcupine Hill. But there was no trace of John or the BMW. Alyssa sat for a moment in her truck, bereft. What had she done wrong? She'd set things right, hadn't she? Why hadn't it worked? Why hadn't John waited for her?

When had she fallen so hopelessly in love with a man she'd never met but knew so well?

Alyssa rushed into the kitchen bursting from her coat and gloves. The dirge no longer played. That confirmed her fear.

Kirsten walked in with a large pan. "Did you find the firewood?"

"Firewood?"

"That's why you went outside. With the roads the way they are you insisted we all stay until the salt trucks go by."

"I did?"

"You even invited anybody to stay the night. How much did you have to drink? Nobody wants to do a sleepover with Tootsie Winters."

Alyssa sort of did. Tootsie was the one person who might explain all this, or at least help Alyssa feel better. She peeked in the living room. There were no ghosts. Just her neighbors. Bob Winters stoked the fireplace.

Alyssa muttered, "John?"

From behind her, Kirsten said, "You heard? Not sure how because Claire just called here."

"Heard what?"

"John Christopherson went back into ICU. They don't think he's going to make it. Something about bleeding on the brain now."

"He's alive!" Alyssa gripped Kirsten by the arms and jumped up and down. "I'm sorry." A trickle of sweat ran down her back. "Can you start some cocoa and serve it?"

"Glad to."

Alyssa hurried to the empty parlor where the casket served as the dessert table. "Sadie? Joette? Moonbeam? Anybody?"

Nobody appeared.

She moved the cemetery cupcakes, bloody eyeball cake, and worm desserts off the casket. When she lifted the lid, she stifled a scream. John lay inside stretched out in a dark suit and tie, his eyes closed.

"John! Stop it! Come back to me. I have to tell you about Rose. And Hank."

He lay still.

A shiver whipped down Alyssa. "You can't do this. I put things to right, more than right. Rose and David needed hope. I gave them their dream back. I know that sounds horribly lofty, but I did. Because of you. You gave me direction for my life. But you and I have tons more work to do."

John didn't move.

She touched his cheek, but her fingertips detected only tepid air. "What about the man in the BMW? You have to save him." She'd try anything to get him to stay on this side of the river.

She swiped at tears. "Damn you!"

Sadie appeared on the other side of the casket. "Must I wash your mouth out with soap?"

"Grandma!" She rushed to hug the woman but of course felt nothing but thick air that smelled of fireplace smoke. "Why are you back and everybody else is gone?"

"They're having a committee meeting about me. I might get to pass over tonight."

"I'll miss you."

"There'll be others. This family seems to have its share of flaws that'll get them stuck in the in-between."

Alyssa motioned Sadie to follow her around the open casket. "You can see him, can't you?"

"Oh yes. He's well-mannered, good for a dance, but why do you care?"

"I care because he's been helpful, funny, and he's made me change."

"Have you told him those things?"

"He's dead. He's refusing to come back."

"His soul hasn't passed on or he wouldn't be lying here in the coffin yet. Get his attention."

"What if he wants to join his daughters more than stay with me?"

"While you were out, we received word his girls became guardian angels. There was something about two children being born in Moonstone within the year who would need them. Of all things, your Uncle Jay repented for stealing horses and he was allowed to take the little girls across the river."

John's daughters were guardian angels for Rose and Hank! Alyssa's brain churned. "How do I get John to stay? Is it selfish of me to even ask?"

"Of course you're being selfish, but we women battle that flaw all the time so I say phfft! Have you told him that you love him and why?"

"I didn't think it fair to bring up the L word if this wasn't going to work. I'm not ready to die, and he's in the in-between."

"Heavens to mergatroid, but how can a romance happen if the people involved don't say out loud they love each other? Shit! I mean, snickelfritz!" Sadie looked up in panic, then with relief. "I think I got away with that one."

Alyssa stepped up to the casket and reached out--Sadie shut the lid. "I'm afraid that won't work. That's only his soul. You have to talk to his brain and heart and body in order to revive them."

"But he's in a Texas hospital. How do I get there in time? And I'm not related. They'll never let me in the ICU."

"I believe they let a fiancée in."

"I'm supposed to tell everybody I'm engaged to a dying man I've never met? Who's going to believe that?"

Sadie shook her head. "Look around at all these people having a good time. Don't you want John to be a part of next year's dish-to-pass party? To know that you were asked to be a Moonstone godmother? If you desire something enough, isn't it worth a little lie that maybe isn't quite a lie? Perhaps you're not John's fiancée now, but if he lives, might you become his bride? And the mother of his child?"

"That's a lot to lay on a man I don't know for real."

"I believe somebody is calling you."

It was Kirsten.

The party had gone quiet. Alyssa asked, "What's wrong?"

"They're flying John Christopherson up to the Duluth hospital tonight so he can be near his relatives when he dies. Peter LeBarron paid for the private plane."

Alyssa bit her lip to stifle a sob.

She headed for the kitchen with Kirsten trailing her. Kirsten said, "Stay here. It's turning into a blizzard out there."

"I need to be with John."

"How do you know him?"

"I...catered his children's birthday party years ago." It was a lie, but it felt okay, as Sadie had counseled.

Kirsten frowned. "You're a caterer? I thought you said you were a card dealer?"

"I am and I love it." She pulled on tall boots. "I used to cook for crowds, but I've discovered I love this dish-to-pass party concept. If John survives, I'll organize the biggest potluck, dish-to-pass event ever seen in Moonstone's downtown square come next summer. We'll have another roasted pig. Your cranberry stuffed mushrooms. And silkie chicken deviled eggs!"

Pink-attired Tootsie in her tiara waddled in. "I'll invite the governor!"

Alyssa hugged the stout woman. "It's a deal!"

Sadie showed up behind Tootsie. "Hurry, dear. It's going to be midnight before you know it."

Alyssa threw herself against the snowstorm, but minutes later found herself stuck behind a slow snowplow all the way to Duluth with the clock speeding past ten.

When she finally arrived at the hospital, she couldn't go inside the ICU to see John, even if she were his fiancée. The nurse told her that a priest was giving John his last rites.

At the sight of the priest coming out of the ICU, Alyssa broke into tears. She slumped onto the sofa in the small waiting area.

Father Lockhart eased down beside her. "Would you like to share a prayer?"

"Is he...?"

"Not yet."

"Where's his family?" It saddened Alyssa to think John was dying alone.

"They're in the hospital chapel."

"Oh." Now she was upset with herself for being disingenuous.

"I suggested they think about John's gifts. What gift did he give you?"

Alyssa sobered. Gift? She stared at her hands, roughened by the work she and John had completed since she'd met him on Thursday. With the dish-to-pass party he'd handed her a new community, a family really, people who had brought her purpose again and a way out of her grief.

Alyssa asked, "Can you really talk to God?"

"We all can. He's a spirit among us."

"I've had enough of spirits lately."

Father Lockhart raised his eyebrows. "What about John's spirit?"

"He's been busy."

"How so?"

"He's been laying tile and sanding floors for me." *Oh how stupid this sounds.*

"You saw his spirit."

She considered his unwavering smile. "I worked beside him. But how is that possible?"

"It's Halloween. We celebrate the dead. Supposedly they rise at this time of year to celebrate. Some of us have faith that rising from the dead can really happen."

"Count me in. But he was also at my house in a coffin, like he was dead again. And now he's in a coma. I have all kinds of things to tell him, but I think I'm too late."

"Never admit defeat so soon. What if you left a message on God's voice mail system for John? Perhaps John is just in a holy restroom or something."

She giggled before she knew what happened. "How does Heavenly voice mail work?"

He cradled her hands in his. "I'm like a cell phone tower. I'll relay your message between here and where it counts. Please leave a message for John Christopherson. Beeeeeep."

Alyssa found strength in the priest's silliness laced with sincerity. "John, hi."

That was a start, but now what? Maybe like Rose, the mother of her lost child, she could now look ahead in life. "We have to finish the house. Next summer, you'll have to help me paint the upper story."

The priest squeezed her hand. "It's okay to be more personal."

Her brain went blank. She'd fought her way through the storm twice tonight for this? "John, what color do you think I should paint the house?"

She cringed, but the priest nodded. "Color is personal, it has emotion. What's his favorite color?"

"I don't know."

"How did he make you feel?"

"He made my life...bright yellow. He was as warm as the sun, too."

The priest patted her hands. "He must have loved you."

Alyssa fought to breathe. "We never had the chance to say those words." *Because I was too afraid to say them.* The revelation struck her like plaster falling on her head at her house.

"Your chance is now." Father Lockhart left for the hospital chapel.

Alyssa got up to leave, too, but then halted. It dawned on her that the priest had purposely left her alone. If she hurried, nobody would know she'd sneaked into John's room.

The clock was pushing eleven.

Chapter 7

Stitches criss-crossed John's bruised face and bald head. His new look gave Alyssa pause. He lay in repose on a shallow pillow, his shoulders peeking out of a sheet. She guessed he was in leg casts. One arm was in a cast. Wires snaking out from under the sheet tethered him to monitors. An IV apparatus stood like a sentinel.

Alyssa edged to his bedside, wondering how this fragile patient could possibly be the robust John she knew.

Perspiration prickled her face and broke out in her palms. By reflex she reached into a pocket and came up with Sadie's hankie with the crocheted *yellow* edges.

"Hey, John. Mr. Sunshine."

She reached out. She was surprised to find his shoulder toasty. They'd outfitted the bed with a warming blanket. No wonder he'd always been humming with heat around her.

She touched the stubble on his jawline. It was itchy. He was real. "John, I can't stay long. Your relatives will be here soon. But I wanted to tell you..."

Where do I begin?

"I need you to stay because I owe you. You gave me the gift of bravery to live my life in a new way, all because you had that silly idea about a dish-to-pass party for my dead relatives. And let me tell you, remembering my relatives has been quite a party. I put all their pictures up on a wall in the house. I come from a motley crew. They're imperfect, every one of them. Like me. They swear, steal horses, and make lime gelatin with shredded carrots and mayonnaise for garnish." She shuddered. "You have to be brave to eat lime gelatin with mayo."

She sank at his non-response. Could she be brave enough to say goodbye? Yes. He didn't deserve to live in pain or be an invalid the rest of his life.

Alyssa backed away, intending to leave, sniffling into the handkerchief with the yellow roses on the edges, when she took a good look at the hankie. She got mad. The last few days had been glorious. She wanted them to continue.

She shook the hankie at him. "Wake up! You're making me ruin this heirloom. I've been crying buckets for you. I might've been hiding out from life, but your flaw was that you kept running away to do death defying construction jobs to tempt fate. Talk about selfish. I need you. Wherever you are now, get your butt back here!"

She marched back to the bed, cupped his chin with the greatest of care, and pressed a hard kiss on his lips. They were cool as a corpse, though. She kissed him again to warm him as he'd warmed her so many times.

To her surprise a tiny grunt emanated from him.

She detected a slight movement under his eyelids.

"Come back, John."

His lips parted. A faint whisper ebbed out. "Who are you?"

Alyssa swallowed her disappointment. "I'm a...volunteer here. Would you like a magazine? I have *Penthouse, Playboy* and *Popular Mechanics* on my cart."

John grunted.

"Come on, John. Stay with me. John? I love you."

He never responded. But Alyssa clung to hope. She went in search of a nurse with the news about him speaking.

The nurse said that momentary glimmers were common for comatose and dying patients.

Alyssa glanced at the clock on the wall. Twelve-ten. To her horror, she wasn't sure if she'd told him she loved him before midnight.

When she finally pulled into her driveway in the wee morning hours, her guests were gone and the driveway plowed. Her heart lifted. She imagined John had done the plowing and shoveled the paths to the doors. He loved to pitch in. She loved him for it.

Inside the kitchen, she stamped her boots on the newspapers put down to collect the melting snow. "John?"

Tootsie Winters, in her pink fairy princess costume and tiara, came into the kitchen carrying a stack of dishes. "That's the last of it."

"You stayed to clean up?" Alyssa fought back tears at the unexpected kindness.

"Hon, it's the neighborly thing to do. How is he?"

Alyssa flinched.

Tootsie put the plates on the counter. She hugged Alyssa. "You tried. That's what's important."

"But he didn't know me."

"That was only his body that didn't know you tonight. You stepped between two worlds. You knew the spirit of a man who was in the middle of making a huge decision. All you can do now is accept his decision."

Tootsie proceeded to wash dishes.

"Do you need a ride home? Where's your husband?"

"He was so impressed with your antiques that he took the key off the hook and went to your barn to look at more. Since retiring he's become obsessed with decorating the yacht with local historical items. I hope you don't mind?"

"Not at all. He can have them all." She'd love to make sure some of that stuff wasn't dragged back into her house by wayward dead relatives. "I'll vacuum the living room. I won't be able to sleep anyway."

"When Bob landed in the hospital I came home and cleaned out two closets. Found an old girdle. It seemed symbolic to burn it. I used to be an uptight woman, in case people haven't told you."

"No, they haven't." Sadie would appreciate the white lie.

"With Bob on his death bed I vowed to let it all hang out. I vowed to change."

"I understand."

"I know you do, hon." Tootsie winked at her.

⁂

Alyssa took extra shifts at the casino. Monday flowed into a bitterly cold Tuesday and John clung to life. It was an awful feeling to know he lingered in the in-between, undecided, unable yet to live a full life on either side of the river.

Early Wednesday, a rapping downstairs stirred Millicent into a "meow". The cat leaped off the bed, eschewing her usual hideout to slip out of the bedroom and thump down the stairs.

The rapping grew louder.

"I'm coming." Alyssa flung on her lavender robe. The house had gone frigid. She wondered if the ancient oil furnace had finally belched its last smelly vapor. She'd ask John to take a look at it--

Or not. She dragged herself downstairs.

In the kitchen Millicent stood fluffed twice her usual size in watch-cat form, staring at the door.

"Who is it?" Alyssa glanced at the clock above the sink. It was only seven o'clock.

When no answer came, she shuffled to the curtains and pulled them aside. She saw nobody.

But when she unlocked the door, in slid a foul-smelling, brown-and-copper mottled cat. "Dillinger?"

He smacked his lips, suffusing the air with the odor of decaying mice. Burrs stuck to his hips like holsters for six-shooters. Alyssa closed her eyes to will him back into her dreams.

But Millicent hissed at him. *For the very first time.*

Alyssa went wide-eyed. "You're real?"

Dillinger arched his back at Millicent. Then he whipped his tail. He whipped it again as if proud of the ugly striped brush matted with burrs.

A rapping at the front door didn't give Alyssa time to think except to leave the kitchen door open to the cold outdoors in hopes the feral cat would run away.

At the front door Deputy Lily Schuster held a mannequin. "I found your guy."

The dummy had dark hair, a camouflage jacket, denims, and red stains on its face, hair and shoulders. Alyssa knew it wasn't her "guy". She'd seen the real John in the hospital. "Come in."

Her cheeks ruddy from the cold, Lily beamed. "This showed up behind the hardware store where it'd been dumped. One of the culprits dropped his cell phone in the snow. I tracked it to a teenager and his buddies. That car rolled, but those teens were playing a prank. Case closed."

Not exactly. Alyssa was sure John had existed in some form in that BMW and in her house. How? She couldn't say. Souls and ghosts had their own rules.

Lily said, "Say, you heard about John?"

"What?" She grabbed at her robe for support.

"Claire hasn't called you?"

"I'll be seeing her at work today. But tell me."

"He woke up. I guess they're saying there's hope for a recovery now. A miracle. He keeps asking for the magazine lady."

Magazines? He remembers me!

The snarling sounds of cats distracted them.

"Crap. That's a feral cat that got in my kitchen just as you knocked on the door."

"I'll help you get rid of him."

"And then I need your help getting me to Duluth in record time."

"Be glad to. It'll be the first time I've used my new squad's siren and lights."

Alyssa found an army of doctors, therapists and nurses in the ICU waiting area. Alyssa's bravery faltered a notch with them staring at her.

The nurse asked, "May we help you?"

"I'm the volunteer who tried to bring him magazines on Halloween. Is he going to be all right?"

A woman who introduced herself as his physical therapist said, "He's got several months of recovery ahead. We'll be moving him to a nursing home soon."

In numb terror, Alyssa blurted out, "He can live with me. I have lots of things he can do for therapy."

The therapist raised her eyebrows. "You're a relative?"

"Yes. No. Maybe."

The army frowned.

The therapist said, "He needs a place equipped with a hospital bed, and other equipment for rehabilitation."

"I've got plenty of room in my parlor." *If I make sure the casket stays out of there.*

"But he'll have to agree to this. It'll be embarrassing for him, possibly for you. There'll be things you may have to do for him that--"

"I have a lot of neighbors I can call on."

The therapist nodded to the others. "It's up to John, I guess."

The doctor allowed Alyssa into John's room. He was awake, but he didn't look much better.

"Hey, John. Remember me?"

"Not really."

She expected that. "I'm the volunteer."

"The one with the *Playboys.* I'm afraid I'm in no shape for centerfolds, but it's always the thought that counts."

She blushed. "How about *Popular Mechanics?* The centerfold of the car engine looked like it could get you up."

He chuckled then winced in pain. "They tell me I was about to die. That would've been a nice way to go."

With a shrug, she said, "A lot of people meet the Maker after sex."

"I meant the kiss. Your kiss."

Now she really did get hot. "You remember that I kissed you?"

"Probably not medical protocol here, but a sweet kiss beats being fed soup by the other volunteers." He winked.

A thrill bolted up her spine and into her hair. Did he remember the other life? She winked back. "They're talking about moving you to a nursing home."

"The next step. Before I get to look at *Playboys.*"

"Now don't answer hastily, but you could come live with me. I have this huge house--"

"Do I know you?"

"I don't know."

"How can you not know? You're not a kook, are you? Like those women who marry guys in prison?"

Stunned, she couldn't think of a thing to say. Then she smiled. She had a new purpose in life and she better get on with it. "Yeah. I'm a kook. And we know each other already. We're friends."

"So my memory's not so good?"

She took a deep breath. She had to put all this in lay terms, something mere mortals like Bob Winters and John would accept. "Did you have any dreams while you were in your coma?" When he shook his head, she got braver. "Yes, you did. You were at a party, in a house with a running toilet that you fixed. That was my house."

"It was?"

"You remember the toilet?"

"Stuff in here gurgles. I dreamt about a toilet, yeah."

"I'll take what I can get. What about a man in a BMW? Did you see him alive?"

He frowned. "Nothing like that in a dream, but one of my docs said he was speeding on his way to get here for me last night and rolled his BMW. Came out of it fine, luckily, but I think it taught him a lesson. He was pretty shaken up."

"Thank goodness you're both all right." She had to smile. The doctor, in being dedicated to saving John, had speeded but had learned a lesson that would likely save him in the future and untold others.

Now for the final test. With fingers shaking, she pulled the special photos out of her pocket. "That's my daughter and those are your girls."

"Where'd you get this?"

"You put it up on the wall of my house. John, you were in my house. You said that someday I might know what my daughter's last words were for me before she died."

He stared at her for a long time. "You're spooking me out."

"I know. But you have to trust me. We knew each other. And I fell in love with you."

He stared at her again, then at the photos. *She knew* he loved her; he just didn't know it yet. "John, I've never done something as goofy as this. You're going to wake up one day and realize you love me and that you feel like you've known me for a long, long time. You have to say yes. You have to try this new life."

He touched his girls' faces, then Sadie Rose's. "I know what she said. Your daughter."

Her heartbeat paused. "You do?"

"It's what every little girl says when she says goodnight. It's always the last thing a little angel says before she goes to sleep. 'I love you, daddy. I love you, mommy.'"

"She said that? You know for sure?" Alyssa wanted to skip about the room.

"For sure. My daughters said that every night before they went to bed."

"My daughter said that, too."

"Then you have to trust she said those words and had no fear before going to sleep the last time. I'll trust you, if you'll trust me."

"I heard that your daughters are guardian angels now."

"And your daughter?"

"I'm not sure. We'll have to find some child who needs one."

She kissed him, letting the heat build and simmer and swirl about them in an aura shimmering with a rainbow of emotions.

When she rose, he caught her with the one hand not in a cast. "Did we used to kiss like that?"

"Always."

She kissed him soundly again, but this time he gave back with a lightning bolt of sizzling razzle dazzle that brought her to her tiptoes.

Catching her breath, she said, "We definitely knew each other before this."

"Well, heavens to mergatroid."

Alyssa cocked her head. "Where'd you hear that? And what the heck does it mean?"

"My father used to love the cartoon character who said it, a cat named Snagglepuss. Are you allergic to cats?"

"No. I have one, a big white fluffy thing. You have a cat, too?"

"A Maine coon cat. A street fighter. Brown-and-orange. Friend of mine in Moonstone's been keeping him. Said he ran away last Thursday."

Thank goodness! "He probably misses you."

"Nah. He runs away every time there's a cat in heat within miles around."

The blood drained from her head. "Oh no."

"Something wrong?"

I left Dillinger and Millicent alone in the kitchen when I talked with Lily. Dillinger's tail was whipping in a peculiar way. A flirting sort of way.

"I think we're having kittens. I think you and I are starting a family."

Alyssa kissed John before he could ask any more questions.

She knew this would work out. She was brave again because of John. She'd reconnect with her mother, find her father, make sure Rose and David thrived, and get John back on his feet. John had helped her find the courage to accept surprises. She could now dare to live in many dimensions, to live fully--no matter how spooky.

She also knew she'd have a dish-to-pass party for her wedding reception. Whenever that would be. They'd have skubanky, reeble, mulgipuder, abenkater, blood sausage, roast boar, succotash, lime green gelatin, macaroni and cheese with catsup, a chocolate layer bridal cake held together with toothpicks...

And love. Heavens to mergatroid, but life was gonna be good again.

She knew.

If you enjoyed this author's book, then please place a review up at the site of purchase, and any social media sites you frequent!

You can find ALL our books up on our website at:

http://www.writers-exchange.com

All our romances:

http://www.writers-exchange.com/category/genres/romance/

All Christine's Books:

http://www.writers-exchange.com/christine-desmet/

About the Author

Christine **DeSmet** is an award-winning fiction writer and professional screenwriter. She is the author of the bestselling *Fudge Shop Mystery Series* and the popular novella series called *Mischief in Moonstone*.

She is a Distinguished Faculty Associate in Writing at University of Wisconsin-Madison where she teaches novel writing and screenwriting and directs the annual summer Write-by-the-Lake Writer's Workshop & Retreat. Through her master classes she has seen many of her adult students become published.

She is also a professional writing coach in the UW-Madison Writers' Institute conference's Pathway to Publication program.

Christine is a member of Mystery Writers of America, Sisters in Crime, Wisconsin Writers Association, Wisconsin Screenwriters Association, and other professional associations.

Christine is active on Facebook and you can also find her at http://www.ChristineDeSmet.com

Christine's author page at Writers Exchange E-Publishing is: http://www.writers-exchange.com/christine-desmet/

If you want to read more about books by this author, they are listed on the following pages...

Fudge Shop Mystery Series

Deadly Fudge Divas

A taste of trouble is in the air when a group of well-heeled, fudge-loving women descend on Ava Oosterling's newly acquired and lovingly refurbished bed & breakfast inn for a chocolate lovers' getaway.

When one of the women turns up dead--and Ava's grandfather is a prime suspect--Ava plunges into the thick of a murder case stickier than her candy store's line of Fairy Tale fudge flavors and the chocolate facials the women adore at the local spa.

It's springtime and the start of the tourist season in Fishers' Harbor, Wisconsin. Ava has opened the Blue Heron Inn with the help of handsome construction worker Dillon Rivers. Unfortunately, Dillon's mother--Ava's ex-mother-in-law--is among the secretive divas who become suspects along with Grandpa.

Ava turns for help from her friends but they have troubles, too. One is eager for a wedding proposal to unfold on live television, while another friend is expecting her first baby and asks Ava to assist with the birth.

Everything and everybody Ava loves seems in chaos--her fudge shop, her inn, her family, and her own friendships... Until she uncovers a thirty-year-old secret of the "deadly fudge divas".

Publisher: https://www.writers-exchange.com/deadly-fudge-divas/

Undercover Fudge

Candy shop owner Ava Oosterling has her hands full when her best friend Pauline Mertens takes a summer job as a wedding coordinator--with the nuptials and reception scheduled in mere days in the back yard of Ava's Blue Heron Inn overlooking Lake Michigan's bay.

To help out her best friend, Ava is intent on making the table favors-- edible fudge lighthouses patterned after their county's 11 lighthouses.

Unfortunately, trying to finish the luscious ruby chocolate lighthouses becomes elusive. The sheriff informs Ava that a band of thieves storming the country may have targeted this wedding. And that's because there's proof Pauline's mother is associated with the thieves.

When the sheriff asks Ava to go undercover, she finds herself in an emotional quagmire. Pauline's mother only recently returned to Fishers' Harbor after years of estrangement from her daughter. And, Coletta Mertens now works as the housekeeper at Ava's inn. Has Ava's fudge-and-wine hospitality provided a hideout for a criminal?

Unfortunately, "until death do us part" takes a murderous twist involving Ava's Grandpa Gil, the dog Lucky Harbor, and Ava's own beau.

Publisher: https://www.writers-exchange.com/undercover-fudge/

Holly Jolly Fudge Folly

An early, deep snow has gifted Fishers' Harbor, Wisconsin, with a perfect setting for the holiday celebration. Unfortunately removing snow from Main Street for the parade reveals the dead tax assessor with a knife in him--containing Grandpa Gil's fingerprints.

It's clearly a setup and one that keeps Ava and Grandpa Gil under the watchful eyes of Sheriff Tollefson. Who wants Grandpa to miss playing Santa Claus in the Christmas parade and why? Who's being naughty instead of nice?

Grandpa doesn't help his case with talk of leaving town for good--words that chill Ava worse than the weather. She can't imagine life without Grandpa's warm hugs and laughter.

When vandals strike the historic shop and someone leaves Ava and fiancé Dillon Rivers for dead in the snow, Ava wonders if she may need the magical help of Santa's elves to solve the holiday folly.

Publisher: https://www.writers-exchange.com/holly-jolly-fudge-folly/
Amazon: https://amzn.to/3ZRZs4C

Mischief in Moonstone Series

Nestled against the sparkling shores of Lake Superior, the tiny village of Moonstone is anything but ordinary. Between romantic entanglements, quirky neighbors, and mysteries that seem to pop up with every season, the locals know life here comes with a generous dose of laughter and surprise. From silkie chickens and a giant prehistoric beaver skeleton to kidnapped reindeer and holiday hijinks, mischief is always waiting just around the corner. Fall in love with the humorous, heartwarming adventures of Moonstone--where romance meets mayhem in the most delightful ways.

Novella 1: When Rudolf was Kidnapped

Crystal Hagan's first-graders are in panic mode. Their beloved holiday reindeer, Rudolph, has been stolen from the school's live Christmas display. Without him, the children are convinced Christmas is canceled.

The trail of mischief leads to Peter LeBarron, the wealthy recluse who lives in a mansion locals call the "North Pole." To Crystal's shock, Peter freely admits to taking Rudolph--but he refuses to give him back without some romantic negotiations of his own.

With the holiday countdown ticking, Crystal must juggle her students' worries, a stolen reindeer, and an unexpected suitor who may have just stolen her heart.

Humorous, heartwarming, and filled with small-town Christmas magic, this novella is perfect for fans of cozy romance and holiday cheer.

Publisher: https://www.writers-exchange.com/when-rudolph-was-kidnapped/

Novella 2: Misbehavin' in Moonstone

Kirsten Peplinski has worked hard to open her dream restaurant on the shores of Lake Superior. But when the men of Moonstone start disappearing in the evenings--and her business suffers--she discovers the shocking reason: a touring boat offering topless entertainment just outside town limits.

Determined to put an end to the mischief, Kirsten confronts the boat's infuriatingly handsome owner, Jonathon VanBrocklin. Instead of backing down, Jonathon kidnaps her--claiming undressing and marriage are the only items on his menu.

Caught between outrage and unexpected attraction, Kirsten faces the wildest adventure of her life. Will she escape this reckless scheme, or discover that true love sometimes arrives in the most mischievous packages?

Humorous, romantic, and funny, cheeky, and charming, *Misbehavin' in Moonstone* is a sizzling small-town escape.

Publisher: https://www.writers-exchange.com/misbehavin-in-moonstone/

Novella 3: Mrs. Claus and the Moonstone Murder

New county deputy Lily Schuster is still learning the ropes when trouble strikes in Moonstone, Wisconsin. On her second day, she arrests archaeologist Marcus Linden for trespassing--only to find herself turning to him for help when a pie contest judge ends up murdered.

The suspects? None other than Henri LeBarron, the town's beloved eighty-four-year-old Santa, and his scandalous new companion, the alluring Felicity Starr. Both women are vying to become "Mrs. Claus" for the upcoming winter celebration--and their rivalry has turned deadly.

With August heat bearing down and tempers flaring, Lily must solve the case, keep her wits about her, and decide if Marcus's kisses are worth more than his alibis.

Quirky, romantic, and full of small-town mischief, *Mrs. Claus and the Moonstone Murder* blends mystery with a heart-stealing romance.

Publisher: https://www.writers-exchange.com/mrs-claus-and-the-moonstone-murder/

Novella 4: When the Dead People Brought a Dish-to-Pass

Three days before Halloween, Alyssa Swain finds a dead man in his car. But when she returns with help, the body has vanished.

Things only get stranger when the supposed corpse--scruffy, tall John Christopherson--appears on her doorstep very much alive...or at least claiming to be. John insists she summoned him to help prepare for a Halloween party, and he refuses to leave her house--or her heart.

But midnight on Halloween looms, and Alyssa must find a way to keep John from crossing into the afterlife forever.

Funny, eerie, and tender, When the Dead People Brought a Dish-to-Pass is a paranormal romance that blends small-town charm with Halloween magic.

Publisher: https://www.writers-exchange.com/when-the-dead-people-brought-a-dish-to-pass/

Novella 5: A Moonstone Wedding

Margie Mueller thought wedding jitters were normal--until her fiancé sent her a fertility rug.

She's no spring chicken, and the idea of raising a brood of Farina babies makes her panic. But before she can call the whole thing off, Tony's boisterous family descends on Moonstone with their parties, opinions, and endless interference.

Then a dead man turns up--wrapped in that same fertility rug. Suddenly, Margie's wedding isn't just in danger of collapsing under family chaos--it's at the center of a murder mystery. And Tony may know more than he's admitting.

Funny, quirky, and laced with small-town mischief, A Moonstone Wedding is a romantic novella with a deadly twist.

Publisher: https://www.writers-exchange.com/a-moonstone-wedding/

Novella 6: The Moonstone Fire

John "Bozeman" Hall has seen it all--longhorn cattle, grizzly hunts, even rattlesnake suppers. But nothing prepares him for Moonstone, Wisconsin.

When a suspicious fire destroys the newlyweds Crystal and Peter LeBarron's farm cabin, Bozeman is determined to track down the arsonist. His first suspect? A young homeless mother and her son, squatting in a cave on the property.

But the closer he gets to the truth, the more Bozeman discovers that danger isn't the only spark in town--so is the pull of unexpected love.

The Moonstone Fire delivers a sizzling blend of small-town mystery, heartwarming romance, and the quirky mischief Moonstone is known for.

Publisher: https://www.writers-exchange.com/the-moonstone-fire/

Coming November 2025...

Novella 7: All She Wore Was a Bow

Kincaid Hunter, professional bull rider and decorated veteran, has never been tamed--least of all by the thought of marriage. But when a good friend back home in Wisconsin plans a Christmas wedding, Kincaid can't resist riding in to try and stop him from making what he thinks is a big mistake.

What Kincaid doesn't expect is to be lassoed himself--by a wedding planner dressed as Mrs. Claus, with a sparkle in her eyes and a bow for every occasion.

Soon, the cowboy who vowed he'd never walk down the aisle discovers that love can tie a knot tighter than any rope.

All She Wore Was a Bow is a festive small-town romance full of humor, heart, and holiday magic.

Publisher: https://www.writers-exchange.com/the-moonstone-fire/

Coming Soon:

Novella 8: Pest Control

Novella 9: The Big Love & Murder Shilly-Shally in Moonstone

You can find ALL our books up on our website at:

http://www.writers-exchange.com

All our romances:

http://www.writers-exchange.com/category/genres/romance/

All Christine's Books:

http://www.writers-exchange.com/christine-desmet/